The coming of the railway is the most spectacular and exciting thing Jem has ever seen. But not everyone is enthusiastic. People don't like change, and they c... don't like the rough gangs of n... hanging around.

But for Jem and his sister, Kate, there's nothing they can do—they're caught up in the middle of the hatred and uneasiness that is surrounding the village. Can they dissolve the tension before it erupts into violence?

'genuinely moving'
 Times Educational Supplement

'This book is a winner.'
 Carousel

GILLIAN CROSS has been writing children's books for over fifteen years. Before that, she took English degrees at Oxford and Sussex Universities, and she has had various jobs including working in a village bakery and being an assistant to a Member of Parliament. She is married with four children and lives in Warwickshire. Her hobbies include orienteering and playing the piano. She won the Carnegie Medal for *Wolf* and the Smarties Prize and Whitbread Children's Novel Award for *The Great Elephant Chase*.

Other titles by Gillian Cross include:

Tightrope
ISBN 0 19 271750 2

'A taut, beautifully written book.'
 Mail on Sunday

' . . . this is Gillian Cross at her best'
 The Daily Telegraph

New World
ISBN 0 19 271852 5

'a tour-de-force . . . Cross's book is more than just a thriller.'
 The Financial Times

On the Edge
ISBN 0 19 271863 0

'A powerful novel'
 Junior Bookshelf

The Iron Way

THE IRON WAY

Gillian Cross

OXFORD
UNIVERSITY PRESS

OXFORD

UNIVERSITY PRESS

Great Clarendon Street, Oxford OX2 6DP

Oxford University Press is a department of the University of Oxford.
It furthers the University's objective of excellence in research, scholarship,
and education by publishing worldwide in

Oxford New York

Athens Auckland Bangkok Bogotá Buenos Aires Cape Town
Chennai Dar es Salaam Delhi Florence Hong Kong Istanbul Karachi
Kolkata Kuala Lumpur Madrid Melbourne Mexico City Mumbai
Nairobi Paris São Paulo Shanghai Singapore Taipei Tokyo Toronto Warsaw

and associated companies in Berlin Ibadan

Oxford is a registered trade mark of Oxford University Press
in the UK and in certain other countries

British Library Cataloguing in Publication Data available

ISBN 0 19 275152 2

1 3 5 7 9 10 8 6 4 2

Typeset by AFS Image Setters Ltd, Glasgow

Printed in Great Britain by Cox & Wyman Ltd, Reading, Berks

CHAPTER ONE

'Grrrrr—on!'

A huge hand thudded down, knocking a cloud of chalky dust from the horse's rump, and the animal lumbered into a trot along the embankment. The navvy holding the bridle ran beside, while the loaded truck gathered speed as it swayed faster and faster after them.

'Whoa there!'

The swerve came like magic, man and horse turning aside in a single practised movement.

CRASH!

With a rattle of earth and rocks the truck bumped the log across the unfinished end of the embankment, tipped up and thundered its load down the slope.

Jem let out his breath and wriggled forward on his stomach to stick his head even farther out of the bushes. The moment never palled. Evening by evening he had watched the embankment grow, driving in a straight line down the valley towards London, and still the noise and movement stirred him as they had the first time.

Behind him was the quiet of the countryside. In the thin light of the October evening the birds flew and the sheep nibbled their way slowly over the Downs as they had done for hundreds of years. But Jem had no eyes for them and no thought for the past as he stared, exhilarated, towards the line. His thoughts were all of the future as he watched the huge navvies bend to their shovelling, with a clatter of metal on stone, bellowing rude jokes and carving their way with pick and spade across the peaceful valley.

He wriggled with excitement, ignoring the thorns which drove through his old smock. It was wonderful to be alive now, when the sleepiness of the past was being shattered by this extraordinary new thing. The Railway. The very word brimmed with action. In his mind he saw dragons, steely and fire-breathing, poised to tear their way up the valley from Helmston to London, and the dirty, foul-mouthed navvies, shining and slippery with sweat, towered like giants in his imagination. In all his twelve years he had never seen men so confident, so untouched by the ordinariness of life.

Another truck set off on its journey along the rails with a jangling of harness, the horse's hoofs scrunching on the loose earth of the embankment top. At exactly the same place as before the horse was unharnessed and jerked aside, just when it seemed that horse and man must go tumbling over the end as well, in a somersault of legs, wheels, and earth.

A sudden cold gust of wind found its way through the bushes and caught Jem at the back of the neck. His mind came back to himself and he felt for the first time the clamminess of the ground seeping through his clothes and the prickles scratching his arms. The grey of the sky was becoming black. It was time to go home.

Home. He sighed reluctantly. Once, not so long ago, it had been warm to think of, good to go back to, but now the memory of it was colder than the evening about him, rasping every nerve with harshness. Still, there was nowhere else to go. He backed cautiously out of the bushes, catching his breath as his worn smock ripped on the thorns, and straightened stiffly. There was no slackening of the noise in the valley. The navvies were working to a deadline and would carry on while there was light to see by, but he dared not stay any longer and, with a last, regretful glance over his shoulder, he set off across the fields.

As he came to the rough lane-end leading to the village, he saw Ben ahead. His friend dawdled along, slicing at the hedgerow with a switch and whistling softly, and Jem walked faster to catch him up.

'Hallo.'

''Lo.' Ben nodded, a smile on his round, freckled face. 'Been working late?'

'No. Been for a walk.' Better not to mention the navvies to Ben. Even Ben. The two boys fell into step and Ben tossed his switch over the hedge.

'Coming up the forge?'

'Could be. Got digging to do though.'

Ben grinned. 'Always at it, you Penfolds. Don't you ever get a day off?'

'Got to eat, haven't we?' Jem's shrug was resigned. It was all right for Ben to talk. Things were easy for him. 'Kate'll skin me if I skive off.'

'*Her*.' Ben glanced at him, knowing and sympathetic. 'She having one of her sour turns?'

'She's one long sour turn.' Jem had no softness for his sister. 'Nag, nag, nag, all day long.'

'My mum reckons she's a wonder,' said Ben with a chuckle.

'She does?' Jem was unimpressed.

'What with you and the baby and all, and her only sixteen. Says she's kept the family together like a proper little mother.'

The word mother made Jem wince, like a touch on a sore tooth, and to cover the movement he snorted. 'She should try living half a day with her. Might not think her such an angel then.'

He gazed morosely down at the road, wanting not to remember his parents. The hard times they had had when his father was there and his mother was alive seemed now like some lost dream, all summer days and rabbit stew. Best not to think. Ben clapped him awkwardly on the back, trying to alter his mood.

'Cheer up. Six years and we'll be men. And won't we show them?'

It was an old dream, he and Ben grown and footloose. Many a happy hour they had spent, lying in the hayfield or leaning on the old bridge, planning their adventures. Sometimes it was to be a shearing gang and sometimes they were to be horse-men, but always together and free to make their choice of all the farms around. But now it seemed as far away as the moon, with six long years of nagging and potatoes in between. And even when the six years were done and he was eighteen, there would still be Kate and Martha to keep, clinging to his back, unable to be left. The dream was bitter on him already, but it was no use to tell Ben. Ben had no troubles of his own. He was still a boy. Beside him, Jem felt a grown man, burdened with worries and responsibilities. How could Ben understand that?

But Ben understood more than he supposed, for he said, softly, 'If she marries, you'll be free of her.'

'Marries?' It was funny enough to disperse his black mood. 'Marries? Her? Now there's a wife for a man. Every bone of her would spike you.'

'She needs a fat one then.' Ben's eyes gleamed with the joke. 'Like Elijah Day.'

'Elijah Day?' Jem looked at him sideways and suddenly they both broke into roars of delighted laughter at the thought. Bony Kate with Elijah Day, the baker, who rolled and rippled with flesh, shaking timidly as his ancient mother screamed at his laziness. Jem felt his heart lighter as they came to the gate of the forge.

'Happen I'll be up later.'

'Right.' Ben turned in at the door of the forge and

4

Jem made his way on to his own home which squatted among the elder trees at the back end of the village. Even now it was the neatest of all the cottages. Neater, perhaps, as though to defy all the misfortunes which had fallen on the Penfolds. He suddenly remembered the rip in his smock and braced himself for a quarrel.

But at the door of the cottage he guessed that he was safe for the moment. He could hear the fat voice of Mary Ann, the Rector's old maidservant, laying down the law inside. Unlatching the door, he slid through and gave a polite nod before sitting down to take off his field boots. But the old woman ignored him, being in full spate.

'—of course he's terrible, with his nervous stomach. The least bother and he's as sick as a dog with it, poor man.'

Poor Rector! Jem grinned down at his boots. Couldn't even be sick without the whole village hearing of it.

'And how's the baby then, dear?' Mary Ann was childless, but she counted herself an expert on babies, as though sheer age had taught her what experience never would.

Kate sat straight on her stool on the other side of the fire and folded her hands together. 'Well enough, thank you.'

Was it three nights or four, Jem wondered, that she had sat up sleepless while Martha screamed? He could not remember, but watching her, rigid and proud, he thought that no one would ever guess. Mary Ann sighed luxuriously.

'It's a cruel thing, I always say, when the Lord takes the mother and leaves the child, but folk like us must not question His wisdom.' She gave a self-satisfied smirk. 'Mrs Neville told me to ask if the cow's milk was agreeing with the little precious.'

'Thank her very kindly,' Kate said stiffly.

'And where is the blessed child? In the cradle? Let me take a look at her.'

Levering herself to her feet with difficulty, the old woman waddled across the room and bent over the cradle.

'Not a bit peaky, is she? A lovely child. You'd think she was a sight more than two months, wouldn't you?'

Jem could tell from the way Kate's foot was jerking that she itched to send the old woman about her business. It was never Kate's way to sit idle for long. The cottage gleamed white and bare, a monument to her incessant scouring and scrubbing. The baby shone pinkly in a way which seemed most unnatural to Jem. It was wash and sweep and scrub all day long, when she was not sewing or cooking, and now she clearly fretted to be at it again. Thoughtfully he flicked a lump of mud from his boot into the fire and gazed at the red shapes, trying once more to imagine a railway engine and what it would look like coming down the valley.

A fierce tweak at the shoulder of his smock brought him back to the scene in the cottage as Kate, scandalized, hauled him up to say goodbye to Mary Ann. Politeness came next to cleanliness in her book and she was always obsequiously polite to everyone from the Rectory.

But as soon as Mary Ann had wheezed and chattered her way through the door Kate rounded on Jem.

'You've no call to take those boots off.'

'Thought you didn't like them inside.'

All he got for his cheekiness was a cuff on the ear. 'Put them on and get yourself into the garden.'

'Aw, Kate, it's near dark out there.' But he was only trying it on. He knew that he would have to go. With a brisk shove Kate sent him through the door and he caught up the spade as he passed. 'Worn down to me knees I'll be,' he muttered. 'Be on show at the fair as a freak.'

But once he started he was glad of it. The ground had to be dug for the beans, and leaving it a day would put him behind. The patch was a sight too big for a boy of his age to work alone, but there was no one else to do it and without it they would starve. Bending to his spade, he pretended to be a navvy, and sent the stony earth rattling so energetically that by the time Kate called him to his tea he had dug over all the bit marked out in his mind.

Warm from the work, he did not feel such a need to annoy Kate and he washed at the well and took his boots off at the cottage door as she liked him to. The pot of potatoes in the middle of the table sent up a friendly steam and Jem sat down and spooned half into his bowl, taking a great dollop of rosemary-flavoured lard to go on them. Other cottagers might have their scrapings of butter, but the Penfolds always had lard from their own pig and, God willing, would have it again next year in spite of all the troubles that had come to them.

Kate clattered down the stairs and through the door at the bottom. 'Maybe she'll sleep tonight,' she said, jerking her head up the stairs to where she had put the baby. Free of the need to impress Mary Ann, she looked tired, brushing the loose strand of hair from her forehead with a reddened hand, but Jem was not deceived by this moment of weakness and he eyed her warily as he munched his potatoes, prepared for an attack.

More slowly than usual, she spooned nearly all her share of the potatoes into her bowl and then slapped an extra helping into Jem's. He knew he should refuse it, but he was too hungry. He just nodded and took another lump of lard.

'Easy with that,' she said sharply. 'We've scarce enough to do us till we kill the pig.'

The piece she took herself seemed ostentatiously small, as though she were reproaching him. They ate in silence for a while and then he saw her eyes flicker to the tear in his smock. Quickly, to get in first, he said, 'I'll start lifting the taters tomorrow evening.'

'You'd best be home earlier then.' Her voice was cold. 'Where were you wasting your time today?'

'I was up Little Piece, hedging with Hoppy Noyce.'

'Don't give me that,' she said scornfully. 'Hoppy Noyce wouldn't work late for the Queen herself. Where've you been?'

The question snapped out like a stone from a catapult and Jem felt his neck grow hot.

'Went for a walk.'

'Did you now? Quite the gentleman of leisure. Where did you walk? Hey?'

'I—' It was no good lying. She had a nose like a foxhound for lies. 'I went up the line. Just to take a look.'

She closed her eyes briefly and put her hand to her forehead. When she looked up her eyes were tired but her voice was as cutting as ever. 'I'll not have you up there. Do you hear? Those men! We've troubles enough in this family without going after more.'

'Where's the harm?' he said stubbornly.

She began to speak slowly, as though to a small child. 'We must keep respectable. Folks are sorry for us now and help us. I'd rather not, but we need it till you're grown. So we have to be careful. There's those would be glad enough to speak against us if they could, what with Dad and all.'

He stopped eating and looked sullenly at her. 'What's Dad got to do with it?'

She had the grace to look faintly ashamed, but she did not apologize. 'What he did was wrong. Against the law.'

'He wasn't the only one! They all do it! It's nothing!' He was shouting now.

'They don't all get caught,' she said icily. 'Nor sent to Van Diemen's Land. You know it's not nothing. It broke Mum's heart and put her in her grave. But it'll not break mine. I'll live it down.'

Jem put his fork down, suddenly sickened, the potatoes feeling a horrible slimy mass in his mouth. How could she be so cold, as if she were talking about strangers? It was their own mother and father. Catching something of his mood, she grew a little gentler.

'I'm grieved too, lad, but it's no good ninnying about it. What's done is done and we must make the best we can of it. Folk that are soft end up in the Union.'

He sometimes wondered if it were ever out of her mind, the grim shadow of the Workhouse. That drove her and she drove him and between them they had scraped a living for the three of them through the summer. But what would happen now the harvest was done and the winter was coming he did not care to think. He would never be able to make a whole day's work, even at boy's wages, through until the spring. Grown men were hard pressed enough these days. Reminded by Kate's words of what he would rather have forgotten, he averted his eyes and said gruffly, 'She bring you any sewing?'

'Mary Ann? Yes.' Kate nodded at a bundle by the fire. 'Making up and mending. Mrs Neville wants it by Sunday.' She rubbed her forehead. 'I'll need to use a candle and start tonight if I'm to get it done.'

Jem felt that he could not bear to sit and watch her spindly figure bent over the work when he had none to

9

do. All her actions seemed to cry out on him for not being a man who could keep them without her endless slaving. He got to his feet.

'I'm off up the forge.'

She sniffed, her gentle mood vanishing. 'You'd be better in bed.'

'Time enough.' He went to the door to get his boots and she called after him.

'Not long. We don't want you turned off tomorrow for oversleeping.'

'Elijah Day!' he muttered under his breath, and felt better at once. As he walked out of the cottage, the tightness in him ebbed away and he felt light, as though he could skip and float along the lane. It was dark now, but the evening smelt good, with the crisp smokiness of autumn, and he flung his head back and breathed it in as he tramped through the village to the forge.

'A crowd tonight,' he thought, coming up to the gate. Time was that the men of the village had walked the mile to The Three Pigs and taken half a pint of beer every now and again, but things were bad at the moment and the forge was a nearer and cheaper place to meet and talk. It was not many nights that some of them did not come to stand by the dying fire and discuss the state of the farms or the state of the country. But the murmur was louder tonight, as though half the men in the village were there.

Ben was leaning on the gate, waiting. He straightened and nodded when he saw Jem. 'She done with you then?'

'Near enough.'

'Bad, was it?'

Some of their quarrel did not bear speaking of to anyone outside the family. Jem picked on the bit that did, even though he did not hope for any sympathy from Ben.

'She thinks I'm a lost soul because I went to take a look at the line.'

A shadow crossed Ben's face briefly, and then he grinned. 'She's feared Elijah Day will get wind of it, and think she's after a navvy.' He bent down and began to collect up the old horseshoes from the mud of the yard. 'Fancy a game?'

It was a ritual question, because they always played it, and Jem held out his hand for the horseshoes without bothering to answer. It was so dark that he could not really see the target, but that was half the fun of it. They could have played blindfold by now. As he sent the first shoe spinning towards the stick at the end of the yard, he heard Ben say, 'Best not tell them in there where you've been.'

'They grousing about the navvies again, then?'

'Worse than ever.' Ben watched critically as though he could see where the horseshoes were landing. 'That was a good 'un, I reckon.'

Jem took aim again. 'What's set them off this time?'

'Two of the navvies over Little Morden way. They've sloped off without paying and left their landlady in the lurch. A widow. There's talk of going after them.'

'Think they will?' Jem crossed the yard to inspect the stick and swore softly when he found that he had only ringed it once.

As he came back, Ben said thoughtfully, 'Not this time.' He began to throw, easily and expertly. 'But something'll come soon. They've been in a fair ugly mood of an evening these three months and more.'

'Load of rubbish.'

'I'm none so sure.' Ben threw his last horseshoe and went to inspect the result. 'Not bad. Three on. How'd you do?'

'One.'

Ben chuckled. 'Need more practice. Want another round?'

'No.' Jem flung down his horseshoes moodily. 'Let's have a listen to what they're saying.'

'You and your navvies.' Ben gave a melodramatic groan. He was only too well aware of how Jem felt. 'What's so good about a parcel of drunken Irish?'

Irish was bog-Irish to Ben. And Papist at that. Funny, if they weren't so threatening. He had no ear for Jem's tales of the work up at the line, being too used to hearing his father the smith going on about what the navvies did when they were not at work. All Ben asked of life was a full stomach and a good laugh. Being the blacksmith's son guaranteed him enough to eat, but the gloomy mood of the villagers at the moment was not to his taste at all and it turned him against the railway. Judging by the monotonous rumble coming from inside the forge, there would be no belly-laughs this evening, only head-shakings and threats. So Ben hung back.

'Aw, Jem, you don't want to go in there. Stop out here in the air. They're jam-packed inside.'

Jem shook his head obstinately. He wanted to hear what the men were saying about the navvies. 'You coming?'

'Might as well,' Ben said reluctantly, as Jem had known he would. He usually fell in with what Jem wanted in the end.

The two of them dropped to their hands and knees and began to crawl in between the boots. The men let them go by tolerantly, one or two aiming jovial kicks at them. Hoppy Noyce, his battered pipe in his mouth, nodded to Jem and grinned, but did not speak because the smith was in full flow. It never paid to interrupt Joe Hamage.

12

He was a vast man, over six foot tall and broad in the shoulders to match, his arms thick with muscle. Set incongruously above this gigantic body was a round pink face crowned by a mop of sandy curls. When he was washed of a Sunday, a stranger might have been deceived by his face into thinking him mild and simple. No one in the village ever made that mistake. Grimy from the forge now, he towered like a tree in the small space and bellowed out his grievance, emphasizing what he had to say by pounding his fist on the anvil as though his hand were made of iron.

'It's not safe for honest women to walk the lanes round here. Not even in the day. A man from over Little Morden way told me his missus was chased half a mile or more into the village. Three of them. All Irish.'

Jem had opened his mouth to say, 'What's that to do with it?' He was furious that all the men were standing there like sheep, nodding their heads and baaing 'Yes' to Joe's every word. But Hoppy Noyce, tapping his pipe out on his boot, caught sight of him and shook his head. Jem's mouth snapped shut. He had learnt already that Hoppy was most often right about things. Unchallenged, the smith roared on.

'A drunken lot of Papists and Chartists. They do what they like at that camp of theirs. Now they've started down here in the valley. It's a scandal to the whole place. And what does Rector do? Nothing. What do the masters do?'

'Aye. You're right. Nothing.' The men muttered, nodding their heads eagerly at each other.

Baa. Baa. Baa. The sounds jumbled in Jem's sleepy head as he stood crowded near the dying fire beside Ben. He wondered confusedly why they did nothing themselves if they were so put out. Why not do something? Then his eyes moved slowly round the forge

13

and he realized why not. There was a handful of young strong men and another handful of wiry middle-aged men. The rest were old men like Hoppy Noyce, or boys but little more grown than himself. Not much to set against hundreds of navvies. Pictures of the men at the line swam past his eyes, huge heroic pictures. Somehow they did not fit the tales the village men were telling, of theft and violence, assault and foul language. It was all too—Jem leaned back and his head fell forwards on to his chest as he dozed beside the fire.

He woke to a stirring in his ribs. The fire was cold and the smith was poking him with an elbow. 'Move yourself, lad. Can't doss down here. Time to be off back to that sister of yours. Reckon she won't be best pleased with all the ash on your smock.' His sneer mocked Kate's tidiness and mocked Jem for being its victim. The boy felt a twitch of anger as he staggered up. Ben caught at his arm.

'Steady on. Nodded off, you did.'

He steered Jem out of the empty forge and over to the gate.

'All right?'

Jem gave a rather shamefaced grin. 'It's like you said. Proper close it was in there. I'd best be off quickly. It's a deal later than I meant to stay.' He let himself out of the gate and then, unquiet, leaned back over it. 'Fierce in there, weren't they?'

Ben shrugged. 'Got good reason.'

Jem did not fancy admitting it 'Tales! Half of them made up, like as not.'

'Tales or true,' Ben pointed out sensibly, 'makes no odds to how angry they get.'

'What can they do? Twenty to a thousand it is.'

For a moment Ben's forehead wrinkled. 'Don't forget

we're your folk. Not them. Or have you taken against us?'

'Don't talk soft,' said Jem, clapping him on the back. 'Village is Village. It's just—'

'Just what?'

'Oh, nothing.' He turned away, unable to explain to Ben how shamed he felt to see the men of the village so weak and stupid beside the navvies. Village was Village and he was Village, but sometimes he wished . . .

'Don't you let Kate catch you coming back at this time of night,' called Ben softly as he turned away.

'None of that.' Jem grinned into the darkness. 'She'll be sleeping like a babe. Dreaming of Elijah.'

Ben's muffled laugh followed him down the lane as he ran towards the cottage. Fair enough to joke, but what *would* Kate say? Already he could hear the rough side of her tongue and feel her fist on his ear.

But to his relief he found that she had gone to bed. The fire was damped down and the cottage in darkness. Safe till morning at least.

He took off his boots and fumbled his way through the staircase door and up the stairs. His half of the attic was cold and, since Kate was not there to see, he left all his clothes on as he climbed into the big bed which had been his parents'. With his knees drawn up to his chin and the blankets pulled tight he tried to make a warm patch for himself, but it was cold and lonely. Until six months ago he had shared this half of the attic with his mother and father, sleeping on a shakedown beside their bed, warmed by their breathing.

From the other side of the thin wooden wall came the sudden cry of Martha, waking in her cradle beside Kate's bed. The child wailed for a moment and then Jem heard Kate get up and begin to walk with her, bare feet quiet on the boards. Gradually the baby's screams

15

gave place to a steady soothing humming, a gentle noise, quite unlike Kate's daytime sawtooth. For a while Jem lay, half-awake and half-asleep, listening to it in wonder. Then, rolling over, he stuffed his fingers into his ears so that he could go to sleep.

CHAPTER TWO

It was about a week later that Jem came home with bad news. No work for him for at least two days. He trailed up the lane with his head down and had almost bumped into the man at the gate before he noticed him.

'Sure now, do you want to knock me off my feet?' the man said with a grin.

Jem stared. Even without the Irish voice it was obvious what the man was. He stood blocking the gateway, not tall out of the ordinary, but square and muscular in his moleskin trousers and old patched jacket. The green-spotted handkerchief round his neck had a lurid brightness and his battered white felt hat sat drunkenly on his head. Jem's mouth fell open, but it was not until he caught the man's eye that he realized he was staring.

'And have you never seen a navvy-man before? Is that it?'

'Up the line,' Jem stammered weakly, awed as though he were speaking to a fairytale giant. The man smiled again.

'But not in the village?'

Jem shook his head, finding it almost impossible to say anything out loud because of the queerness of it—a real navvy, straight from the line, standing there solid and bright and leaning on their gate as though the cottage belonged to him. It was exciting and frightening, both at the same time, and although the navvy was not extraordinarily big—not the size of Ben's father—he loomed massively against the setting sun, more vivid than an ordinary person.

He stood patiently for a while, smiling quietly as Jem stared, but at last he said, with a nod towards the sty, 'A grand pig you've got there. I've not seen the like of him since I left Kilkenny.'

Jem smiled and shuffled his feet. The pig was a small triumph for him and Kate. It had been a struggle to feed it in the last six months and several times they had feared they would have to sell it half-grown, but it still grunted and rooted in the sty, almost ready to be slaughtered now. Jem grinned at the navvy's praise, cursing himself for a fool because he could not speak out sensibly. He was so embarrassed that he did not realize that the Irishman wanted something until he said, 'Will I come in and have a look at him then?'

'I don't—'

'Sure, there's only the one of me and I'm not wanting to do you any harm.'

This was said with a broad grin and Jem suddenly realized that the man thought he was afraid, that it was terror that trapped his tongue. Pulling himself together he said gruffly, 'Come in,' and pushed the gate open.

They leaned against the ramshackle wall of the sty and the man scratched the pig's back with a switch, crooning endearments to it.

'And aren't you the lovely one? The finest pig this side of Ireland.'

Jem felt uneasily that there must be more to it, that the navvy must have had another reason for coming in. Had he done right, bringing a strange navvy into the garden? And where was Kate? He would have expected her to bounce out at the sound of their voices. He watched the man cautiously as he bent over, his face crinkled with pleasure, smiling at the pig.

At last he straightened and turned to Jem, holding out a huge hand with the brown hair crisp on the back.

'Maybe it's time I introduced myself. Conor O'Flynn from Kilkenny. At your service.'

'Jem Penfold.' Jem's hand was engulfed in the navvy's massive, iron-hard fist and he found the courage to look up. When he did, he met two bright blue eyes which watched him with gentle amusement.

'And now we're introduced, Jem Penfold, perhaps you'll be helping me with my little problem?'

'W-what can I do?'

'It's like this. I'm looking for somewhere to lodge and I've a fancy to live in this village. Would you know of anyone now who might have room for a navvy that's quiet and respectable?'

The conversation at the forge was still fresh in Jem's head and he had opened his mouth to say 'No' when an idea slid into his mind, an idea that was sensible and exciting, both at the same time.

'Can you wait a minute, Mr O'Flynn?'

'And haven't I all the evening? Just you leave me here with this pig of yours and I'll be as happy as the King of Spain at Christmas.'

Jem dashed into the cottage. He found Kate out at the back in the lean-to scullery, scrubbing the floor for all she was worth. Her red elbows pointed sharply outwards and her brown hair was falling out of its stringy bun. The bad-tempered clattering she gave to the pail told Jem why she had not heard their voices out by the pigsty.

'Kate!'

'Get your muddy boots off my clean floor,' she said, without looking up.

'Aw, Kate, this is *important*!'

Slowly she sat back on her heels and drew a thin forearm across her face, waiting. Jem took a deep breath, knowing that she would need persuading, and then in his agitation said quite the wrong thing.

19

'There's a navvy in the garden.'

'What!' She jumped up. 'What's he doing?'

She would have made for the door, but Jem caught at her sleeve.

'Stop. I've not told you. He wants lodgings.'

'And?'

'I thought . . . maybe . . .' His voice faltered away at her outraged look.

'You must be mad, Jem Penfold! The likes of us can't afford to have a navvy in the house. Not if we want to stay respectable.'

'You can't *eat* respectableness!' he shouted, suddenly furious. 'And I've got no work tomorrow. Nor the next day.'

As soon as he said it he saw that was where he should have started. She leant back against the wall as though she had been winded and frowned, thinking hard. Jem pressed his advantage.

'Stands to reason it's going to happen. Now harvest's over I'll not get a full day every day. Happen I won't get a full day every week. We *need* something else.'

She said nothing and he tried again.

'He looks to be very quiet.'

Still silence.

'He could share the big bed with me. There's room.'

He could see her face grow thoughtful, working it out.

'Aw, Kate, he's *waiting*!'

At last she gave a heavy sigh. 'I don't know what's for the best. Have him in then. But no promises, mind.'

Jem bounded joyfully to the door and she called after him, 'Leave me two minutes to put on a clean apron.'

Mr O'Flynn was still talking to the pig and his soft voice mingled with the rustlings and snufflings from the sty in a pleasant, restful way.

'Mr O'Flynn.'

The navvy did not look up at once.

'Mr O'Flynn?'

'That's me.' He said it with a faint smile, almost as though it might not have been.

'My sister says—' What had she said exactly? 'She says will you step inside and have a word with her?'

'I was thinking perhaps your mother—'

'There's only Kate and me,' Jem said woodenly. 'Come in.'

He had a strange feeling, almost as though he were showing their cottage to the Queen, and as they went in he looked at it as if he had never seen it before, trying to guess what the Irishman was seeing. Everything was very clean. The wood was scrubbed white, the brick floor was scoured and the baby slept, pink and shiny, in the cradle. But it was a bare house with none of the fancy bits the other cottages had, no rag rugs, bright tin trays or pictures on the walls. Kate herself, standing in front of the scullery door, was the same, her clean apron spotless, her hair tidied and her back as straight as the poker. But no softness in her face, no welcoming smile.

'This is my sister Kate, Mr O'Flynn. And my sister Martha,' he added, seeing the Irishman's eyes on the cradle.

'Good evening, Mr O'Flynn.' Kate bent her head forward stiffly.

'Good evening to you, Miss Penfold. A fine cottage you have here.'

Her face did not move. 'You're looking for lodgings?'

The rigid politeness in her voice did not deceive Jem. He knew her well enough to tell that the navvy had not impressed her, and he stared at him, ignoring the conversation, in an effort to see what she was seeing. At first he could not. He saw the Mr O'Flynn he had found at the gate, brightly dressed and friendly, smiling at

Kate with cheerful openness. But then, as though it were a perfectly ordinary thing to do, the navvy turned and spat into the fire and the strangeness of it in Kate's clean cottage gave Jem a kind of jerk. For a moment, he saw what Kate saw. A huge stranger, unshaven and none too clean, the white felt hat still on his head, but pushed back now so that he could scratch the front of his scalp as he talked. His old coat was thick with chalky dust and his big boots were odd, one brown and one black. Jem's own working clothes were old and worn, but they were well-cared for, darned and patched. The navvy looked as though his clothes were falling off him and he did not care. Now, as Kate asked him to sit down, he thumped on to a chair and put his feet in their odd muddy boots up on the scrubbed wooden table. He obviously thought that there was nothing in what he did to upset anyone, for he gave Kate a broad friendly smile. Only now Jem could see that the smile would seem rude and over-friendly to Kate. His heart sank. She would never be able to put up with someone like Mr O'Flynn, even though he meant no harm.

At that moment, the baby started to cry. Kate tried to ignore her and go on speaking, but the wails set into a rhythm and distracted her attention. She faltered.

'See to the child now,' Mr O'Flynn said easily. 'I'll do fine with the boy here until you've finished.'

'I—' Kate was about to protest, but the baby shrieked even louder, purpling in the face, and she gave in. 'I'd best feed her now. I'll have to take her upstairs. She'll never settle to the bottle with strangers here. Jem, make Mr O'Flynn some tea and keep him company.'

Carefully she fetched the precious china feeding-bottle that Mrs Neville had given her and filled it. Then she stuffed a twist of clean rag in the top for the baby to suck through and tucked her, still screaming, under one arm. As she went through the door at the bottom of the stairs, she pulled it shut after her, but the weak catch gave and it swung silently open so that they could hear the sound of her feet plodding slowly up the stairs.

Mr O'Flynn turned to Jem. 'She's a fine-looking woman.'

'Kate?' Jem was so astonished that his mouth fell open.

'And who else would I be meaning? A fine woman. She has a colour on her like the rose of summer.'

'But—' Jem was speechless. Kate, to him, was sharpness itself. As she swept past he had felt the breeze from her like a hoar frost. It did not seem possible that *she* could look different to anyone else.

While he stood there, amazed, she began to sing upstairs. He knew that she always sang to Martha while she was feeding her. The baby was difficult and needed soothing. But he had never listened before. Now, his mind still shaking with the notion that the Irishman might find Kate good to look at, he heard her voice freshly as it floated down through the door she thought was shut. It was thin, like a boy's voice, but clear and true, as his mother's had been, and the song it sang was one of his mother's, a languishing ballad of a girl who followed her lover to sea in the disguise of a sailor and was drowned in a storm. Jem shuddered. That voice could not have anything to do with his pinched sister. It was a ghost's voice.

'A fine voice,' said the Irishman softly, almost as if he were contradicting. 'The voice of an angel, to be sure.'

Looking at him, Jem saw that he was blinking hard and that the corners of his eyes were glittering suspiciously. Embarrassed, he got up and shut the door, cutting off the sound of the singing.

'Will you take a cup of tea, Mr O'Flynn?'

'I will indeed,' said the Irishman, with a little shake of his shoulders, as if he were trying to wake up. As Jem hurried to the well, lugging the heavy kettle, he saw him begin to rummage in his pockets. Looking for a pipe to smoke? Jem sent up a quick prayer that it was not chewing-tobacco he was searching for. Kate would never stand for a lodger who spat tobacco juice. He began to wind the bucket down into the well. Perhaps it *was* a pipe, he thought hopefully, and perhaps Kate *would* let Mr O'Flynn come and lodge with them. And then . . . And as he bent to the winch, heaving up the full bucket, he started to daydream about having Mr O'Flynn to live with them, hearing him talk about the line, maybe even . . . Hardly looking at what he was doing, he filled the kettle from the brimming bucket and set off back to the house. As soon as he got near the door he knew that he was wrong about the pipe *and* about the tobacco. It was something quite different that the Irishman had been looking for. He held a little silver whistle to his lips and was picking out, plaintively, the tune that Kate had sung. But when he saw Jem at the door he changed at once, plunging into a breathless Irish jig, his fingers twiddling over the holes of the little pipe so fast that they looked as if they would tangle. As Jem heaved the big kettle on to the hook over the fire, he felt it was holding him to the ground. Without it, he would have been capering round the room in time to the rollicking tune.

The Irishman set down his pipe and grinned at him. 'Did you ever hear the like of that, then?'

'It's good. Play some more.'

But the Irishman shook his head with a smile and put the whistle back into his pocket.

'Later maybe. It's talk I fancy now. Tell me some more of yourself and your sister. Are you all alone, the two of you? With the baby?'

Jem sat down awkwardly.

'Yes.' He was not used to being questioned. All the villagers had known him since he was born and he had never had to explain himself before. Where to begin? He almost gave up before he started, but the Irishman looked kind, asking out of interest not prying, and so he tried.

'My mum—she died two months ago. More than two.'

The Irishman was looking at him carefully. 'When the baby was born?'

'That's right.' Jem studied his boots. 'My dad, he's still alive.'

'Walked out, did he?' Mr O'Flynn was sympathetic, but Jem gave him a furious glance.

'He never would!'

'I beg your pardon, lad. But he's not about?'

Jem looked down again and answered gruffly. 'He's in Van Diemen's Land.' When there was no reply, he continued quickly, 'They all do it, the village folk. They all poach. It's hard living else for some of the big families. But my dad—'

The navvy ended the sentence for him. 'But he was caught?'

'That's right. Transported. Six months ago.' Thinking of it still made a lump in Jem's throat that almost choked him. More to distract the Irishman from his questioning than for any other reason, he asked, 'You been long on the railway?'

'Ten years, boy. Ten long, weary years, ever since I was fool enough to grow sick of my own place and cross the Irish Sea.'

In spite of his words there was pride in his voice and, looking up, Jem saw that he was smiling.

'You like it?'

'Did you ever hear, now, of an Irishman that liked work?' But the blue eyes were full of laughter. 'No, lad, it's been a grand life. Not the camps, to be sure. They're no place for a man that wants to stay decent and save his money. It's all drinking and randies up there. But the *work*. That's something different now. There's a thing for a man to be proud of.'

'It's hard,' Jem said thoughtfully, remembering all the muscles he had seen tensed, all the gleaming sweat and hard-drawn breath.

The Irishman leaned forward eagerly. 'It's not the hardness makes it grand, boy. It's what we're building. Have you ever put your mind to thinking what a fine thing that is?'

Jem wanted to say 'Yes', but he had no words to tell the feelings that the railway woke in him and he let the man sweep on, his eyes fiery and his hand flourishing wide.

'You wouldn't credit it, lad. Till you've seen the speed and the fire of a great engine on its way you don't know what men can do. Think of the places you can travel and the people you can see when the railway's built. For it's not for grand folks only, but for you and me, for parcels and letters, for sheep and cattle. Sure, it will change the land before you're grown.'

Jem felt as he did when he watched the navvies, when he saw the line striking across the valley, and he leaned forward excitedly. 'How? How will it change?'

'Who can say? Who can tell what will happen? It will carry the folk from one end of this land to the other. Have you ever seen a man from Yorkshire now? Or Scotland?' Jem shook his head. 'Of course not. But you will. And London. Sure, you've not lived until you've seen the great city, with her lights shining into the night and her people crowding the streets.'

'Maybe we'd do well to rest content with what we have.' Kate's sharp voice sliced into their excitement. Neither of them had heard her footsteps on the stairs and now they shrank back into themselves at the sound of her disapproval.

Maybe she felt herself that she had been rude, for she moved over to the fire and, unhooking the kettle, began to make the tea, measuring the precious leaves as carefully as she could without appearing mean. Mr O'Flynn watched her, a smile lurking at the edges of his mouth. Obviously, now that he was over the shock of her sudden appearance, he found her amusing.

'You've no love for the railway then, Miss Penfold?'

Kate answered briskly, without looking up. 'It's brought us nothing but roughness and trouble. We're settled folks, Mr O'Flynn.'

He inclined his head, admitting her complaint. 'We're not always all we might be, to be sure, we navvy-men. But we're not here for ever. And think what we'll leave when we go.'

Kate sniffed, sour and disbelieving. 'We're none so fond of strangers. And from what I hear of London we'd do well to keep our distance.'

The Irishman opened his mouth to argue, but as she put a cup of black tea in his hand he seemed to change his mind, sipping his tea quietly for a while. When his cup was empty he spoke again.

'It's plain you've no fancy for navvies, Miss Penfold. How would it be if you forgot my job? There's many can tell you I'm a quiet respectable man. And it's quiet respectable lodgings I'm after.' And he flashed his broad smile at her.

But it was no use. Kate folded her mouth primly. 'I'm sorry, Mr O'Flynn. You can see this is a small cottage. I think you'd do best to ask elsewhere.'

27

The Irishman studied her gravely. Then he said, 'Maybe I'll be leaving you a while to think it over. I've taken a kind of fancy to this cottage, and to your young brother here. You give your mind to it for a day or two.'

'I'm afraid you'll find I don't change my mind,' Kate said.

But he only smiled again. 'If you want me in the next day or two, just you send the lad here up to the line with a message. He'll find me with the gang up at the cutting. Good evening to you, Miss Penfold.'

And he tramped out at the door, whistling merrily. As soon as the sound of his steps had faded, Jem turned furiously on his sister.

'Are you soft in the head? What shall we do? How can you turn away the chance of honest money when there's nothing to tell us if we'll eat this winter?'

Kate turned her face away and muttered, 'He's no lodger for the likes of us.'

'What's so fine about the likes of us then, that we go picking and choosing?' He was enraged at her stupidity, enraged that her finicking had lost him a link with the railway and sent away the solid, friendly navvy.

But still she did not give him back anger for anger. Instead, she tried to ridicule the Irishman. 'A man like that! Spitting everywhere and scratching himself. His head was *alive*, I'll be bound.'

'Hoppy Noyce spits and scratches just like that,' said Jem defiantly. 'You talk to him all right.'

She snorted. 'Talking's one thing and lodging's another. I'd not have Hoppy Noyce lodging in this house either, I can tell you.'

'Hoppy Noyce is a good man!' Jem could tell from the way Kate was speaking, from the way she was not getting angry, that she was none too happy herself about what she had done. But he did not know how to turn her mind, to argue with her. He just got angrier and angrier himself. 'If Hoppy Noyce isn't good enough for you, there's no pleasing you.'

She bent her head wearily on to her hand. 'Maybe. But I've the task of bringing you up, you and the child, and you must be brought up decent.'

'*I'm* no child,' he shouted at her. 'Who is it brings home half the money or more?'

She looked at him with unexpected gentleness. 'You're a good boy and you've had a lot to bear. Trouble's come to you young.'

But her kindness was harder to bear than anything. Jem felt as though she were forcing him, trying to make him understand her problems and weigh him down. He clung on to his rage.

'Anyway, you're wrong about Mr O'Flynn. He's a kind man. Said you were like the rose of summer.'

'He said *what*?'

This time Jem was rewarded by the confusion on her face. He searched his mind for a parting shot and, as he picked up the spade to go and dig the garden, he found one. Looking back at her pink face, he shouted, 'You *deserve* to marry Elijah Day!'

CHAPTER THREE

The next morning Jem woke with the same troubles still in his mind. When he was a child—six months ago—worries had been swept away at night and he had woken every morning to a new, unspoilt day, but now he must carry the worries on himself and the dullness of the October day was grey in him as he opened his eyes. No work. No money. No food. And Kate had flung away the amazing chance that had come to them.

He lay in bed and tried to be angry, but the greyness was too strong. All he could do was pull on his breeches and his old smock and trail downstairs.

Kate was already crouched by the fire, her needle hand bobbing back and forward while her foot rocked the cradle where Martha screamed.

'Got up at last, have you? There's the water to get in.'

He was glad of the work and filled the pot over the fire and the big jug in the scullery almost without drawing breath before he ate his breakfast. Once Kate tried to speak of what had happened the day before, but he cut her short. What was done was done.

Or so he thought. But he had reckoned without Mrs Neville. She came sailing up the lane at about eleven o'clock, while he was digging in the garden. He saw the grey plumes of her bonnet nodding over the hedge, Miss Ellen's plain little hat gliding along behind, and he raced into the cottage to tell Kate. But there was no time to say more than 'Mrs Neville—' before the lady herself gave an authoritative rap on the door and swept in, her monumental body shaking with a briskness that set all the jet ornaments on her dress wobbling and winking.

'Good morning, Catherine.' She plumped down on to the stool in a businesslike way, her crinoline engulfing it.

'Good morning, ma'am.' Kate bobbed a curtsy, her head meekly bent. 'Good morning, Miss Ellen.'

Miss Ellen, having slid in almost unobserved in the wake of her enormous mother, was standing diffidently in the doorway, holding her reticule in front of her with both hands. 'Perhaps she's got a nervous stomach too,' thought Jem. And then almost giggled. At this rate, a shock would set half the Rectory puking.

'I've near finished the sewing, ma'am,' Kate began apologetically, but Mrs Neville flapped an impatient hand at her.

'That's Mary Ann's concern, not mine. She tells me you do well enough. How's the baby?'

It was an order, not a question, and Kate picked Martha from the cradle—where she had just fallen asleep—and handed her to Mrs Neville. The Rector's wife took her as though she had been a parcel.

'H'mm. Looks well, I suppose. Doesn't she, Ellen?'

She thrust the baby up at Miss Ellen, who took it unhappily and stood with it clutched in her arms as though she were afraid it might fall to pieces.

'And the place is clean, I see.' Mrs Neville looked round offensively, with what was meant to be flattering approval. Then she suddenly fired out an accusing question.

'What's all this rubbish I hear about navigators?'

'Navigators?' Kate's confusion was half real and half assumed.

'Fiddlesticks, girl. Don't you be missish with me! Navvies. I hear you had one round here yesterday.'

'There was a man came by last evening,' Kate said, her voice carefully neutral.

'And you had him in, I hear, and gave him tea.' Mrs Neville's rosy face grew a shade purple. 'What were you thinking of, girl? You're not a baby. Whatever would the Rector say?' Mrs Neville always used the Rector as a threat, ignoring the fact that he was the mildest man on earth.

Kate stood in silence. She looked sullen, but Jem guessed that she was really waiting, preparing herself for the next onslaught. Mrs Neville had no understanding of the fear she brought on people.

'Come on, girl! I've kept a friendly eye on your family since that disgraceful business of your father, and I've done what I could for you since your mother passed away. I can't have you mixing with all the riff-raff that chooses to set foot in this village.'

At that moment, Martha set up a sudden wail, having decided that Miss Ellen's arms were no place for a baby, and she distracted Mrs Neville for an instant.

'Goodness, Ellen, what *are* you doing with that child? Give it to me.'

Thankfully Miss Ellen handed the baby back, and her mother propped the child against one jet-encrusted shoulder, rubbing and patting with a practised hand. Either soothed or cowed, Martha grew quiet, but her brief outburst had given Kate time to collect her thoughts and she spoke softly, her voice well under control. Only Jem could see her bony hands clenching fiercely behind her back.

'We had a man from the line ask for lodgings last evening. That's all.'

'And you sent him on his way.' Mrs Neville spoke as if anything else would have been unthinkable.

Kate's flat cheeks grew faintly pink. 'I told him I would think on it.'

Jem looked at her quickly, but she avoided his eye.

Mrs Neville's face flushed as though all her blood had rushed into her head.

'Think on it? Good gracious, girl, you're not serious?'

Kate stared at her feet. 'These'll be hard times for us, ma'am, these months coming. Not much work for boys of a winter.'

'Haven't I seen to it that you've had sewing to do?' Mrs Neville gave an impatient sigh. As if it were a favour, Jem thought sulkily. Where in the village would she get it better done, then? But Kate kept her eyes lowered. She had the trick of meekness better than he did.

'You've been very good—'

'I'm glad to see you're grateful.'

'—but,' Kate went on, as though she had not been interrupted, 'happen there's need of something more. To fetch us through the winter.'

'Well, I've told you what you should do. More than once.'

'Ma'am?' Kate said, her voice polite and her face pale.

'It's the only sensible thing to do and you know it as well as I do. Stop being stubborn and send the baby away. I can find you a family will take her in and welcome. Then you can go into service and one of the farmers will take the boy to live in.'

It was the first Jem had ever heard of the plan, and he stood open-mouthed, but to Kate it was obviously an old enemy. She answered calmly but deliberately, 'I'll not ask anyone else to keep my family while I've breath to do it myself.'

'Hoity toity! There's none so proud as poor and proud.' Mrs Neville tumbled the baby into Kate's arms and rose magnificently to her feet. 'You'll come to it in the end, mark my words, and think yourself lucky to have the chance. And I'm not sure your young brother will thank you for putting it off.'

Kate bit her lip but said nothing and Mrs Neville looked her briskly up and down. 'Please yourself,' she said at last, with a shrug. 'I'll not waste any more words on you. If you're not too proud to take it, I'll send you another bundle of sewing tomorrow.'

'Thank you, ma'am.'

'And let's have no more of this navvy nonsense. A girl your age! The Rector would be appalled.'

'I may not be as old as you are, Mrs Neville, but I'm old enough to choose my own way. I'll do as I see right.' Kate spoke quietly, but there was no mistaking the defiance in her voice. The Rector's wife stared at her for a moment in utter amazement, round-eyed and fuming, and then she rustled out through the door without another word.

Miss Ellen did not immediately follow her. She hovered in the doorway with her eyes on Kate. But as she leaned forward to speak, an outraged 'Ellen!' sounded from the garden and, with a faint gesture of helplessness, she followed her mother.

As soon as their steps had crunched down the path Kate sank to a stool with the baby on her lap. She was shaking all over. Jem grinned at her.

'That was grand! It's time someone told her she doesn't own the village. She thinks it's charity to let you stitch her drawers for her.'

But Kate did not fall in with his mood. 'No, lad. It's a bad day's work I've done and we'll maybe suffer for it. It's no game to be at odds with your betters.'

'Betters!' Jem scoffed. 'She's nothing but a stupid, fat old woman.'

'Stupid or not, it's her money will keep us through the winter. She's right. We've no room to be proud.'

She spoke without fire, totally dampened, and Jem shifted uneasily. He did not like to see her weakness.

'Aw, Kate—'

'But she *does* keep us. What else is there?'

'Take Mr O'Flynn as a lodger!' He clutched at her shoulder in his earnestness. 'If we've that and the sewing and my half-days there'll be no one has a right to tell us what to do.'

He could feel her wavering in the sudden tenseness of her shoulder, and he clutched harder.

'Kate?' There must be a way to persuade her. 'She'll take the baby else. In the end.'

Kate looked up at him. 'And do you want that?'

He had not really had time to wonder, but now he realized that he did not, that this home was better than none, Kate and Martha better than no family. He grinned down at her.

'I'll be off then? Up the cutting?'

She nodded, but without smiling, not quite at ease in her decision yet, and he scrambled through the door before she could change her mind.

As he hurried out of the village, the sun suddenly came from behind a cloud, flooding the Beacon and the valley with colour and filling him with hope and excitement, so that he went on at a run, more from happiness than from urgency.

In fifteen minutes he was standing bewildered at the end of the cutting. Noise filled his ears and his eyes swam with the confusion. Gangs of men, all up and down the workings, chanted and swung to their own rhythms and the steep chalk walls shut in the sound so that it rang deafeningly from side to side. Jem stared, wondering if it was possible to find a single man among the chaos.

'Move your bum, then!'

A barrow crashed into the back of his legs, nearly toppling him to his knees, and a furious navvy flapped him to one side. Jem jumped out of the way.

'I'm trying to find—'

'Good luck to you!' The man pushed by, not stopping to listen, and Jem began to wander down the cutting on his own, getting jabbed by the butt-ends of shovels and sworn at by the shovellers. No one took any more notice of him than that. There were men everywhere—on the floor of the cutting, up at the top, shuttling back and forth between the two. Dazed by it all, he slowed to a stop and spun round, trying to take it all in.

Close by his ear a thick chuckle suddenly broke in, making him do another turn.

'It *is* a boy, then,' said the voice in mock surprise. 'Thought it was a spinning-top I did.'

A wiry man was sitting on a rock in the middle of all the turmoil, calmly drinking a mug of beer. His head was as bald and shiny as a peeled egg, except for a long fringe of ginger hair at the back and over the ears, and a bushy ginger moustache over the mouth. He wiped the white froth from this moustache with an expression of contentment, and Jem felt bold enough to speak to him.

'I'm trying to find a navvy.'

The man chuckled again. 'Won't find any of those here. *Oh* no.'

Jem felt himself go red. 'He's called Mr O'Flynn.'

But that only made it worse. This time the navvy laughed aloud, almost falling off his rock.

'Mister, did you say? *Mister*? That was no navvy, boy.' And he wiped the tears from his eyes.

Jem was beginning to despair of ever getting a straight answer. 'He's called Conor O'Flynn. And he's Irish.'

'You . . . don't . . . say.' The ginger eyebrows went up in pretended astonishment. 'Listen, lad, they're all Irish here but me and Pigtail. And as for names—well, now. Is it Saucepan you want? Or Pegleg? Or Cats' Meat?'

Jem searched his mind, but he could think of only one more thing. 'He plays a penny whistle.'

'*Oh!*' Recognition broke like a sunbeam over the ginger man's face. 'You mean Kilkenny Con! Oh well, that's an easy one. He's up on the last barrow-run. Up the end of the cut. Here, I'll take you.'

Jem stumbled after him, his feet uncertain on the loose ground of the cutting floor, choking from time to time as a cloud of dust billowed up. It was plain to see what the ginger man meant by 'barrow-runs'. At intervals along the cutting, planks sloped up the steep sides and up the planks, delicately balanced, navvies pushed top-heavy barrows of rocks and earth, helped up by ropes pulled from the top. More than once as he and Ginger passed along, Jem saw a barrow wobble dangerously and caught his breath, but no one else took any notice except the navvy actually pushing who quickly righted the load.

When they reached the end, the highest part of the cutting, he saw Mr O'Flynn at last, poised half-way up the run. Without ceremony, the ginger man bawled, 'Kilkenny!'

Automatically the Irishman turned his head, and the movement set his barrow lurching so wildly that it seemed as if it must certainly plunge off the plank and bury him in a landslip of rocks. With a visible effort, he managed at last to set it straight and then, more cautiously this time, he looked back over his shoulder and bellowed a very crude word. The navvies round the foot of the run shook with laughter and one of them slapped Jem's guide on the back.

'Sure, you want your head looked at, Ginger. Kilkenny's no man to be playing silly games with.'

Ginger did not look in the least put out. 'He's all right. Like to keep you all on your toes up this end, don't I?'

'Well, and I hope you're on yours, man. Here he comes back again.'

And so he did. Having disappeared briefly over the top of the cutting, he was now running down at a heart-stopping speed with the empty barrow. As soon as his feet touched bottom he leapt off and seized Ginger by the scruff.

'You English dwarf! Do you want me to take you up in the barrow now and tip you out from the top? Is that it then? Or would you be fancying something slower?' And he went on to detail what else he would like to do to him.

But nothing seemed to abash Ginger. He waited until he was put down, smoothed his fringe of hair and said coolly, 'Must have taught the boy something, that lot.'

'Boy?' Glancing round, his attacker suddenly caught sight of Jem. 'Heaven help us, is it you, boy?'

Jem stepped forward. 'Mr O'Flynn—'

'God love you, will you stop that? You'll have me the laughing-stock of the whole line. Con's my name. Kilkenny Con, if you've a fancy for something grander.'

'Con,' Jem felt the word awkward on his tongue, 'there's a message. From my sister.'

The rude laughter that greeted this unsuspecting remark took him quite by surprise. The men dug Con in the ribs and slapped him on the back.

'Oy-oy-oy!'

'Faith, it's the quiet ones are always the worst.'

'And haven't they warned you about these Sussex girls?'

But Con remained perfectly solemn and, when he could make himself heard, he said calmly, 'You keep your tongues off the lady now. She's a decent woman and not for the likes of you to make game of.'

Jeers and more laughter greeted this and Con drew Jem to one side.

'What is it now?'

Jem was hot with embarrassment and he muttered the message almost under his breath. 'She says it's all right.'

'The lodging?' Con asked quickly. 'Is it the lodging you mean?'

Jem nodded.

'She's changed her mind? You're sure that was the message now?'

'Of course.' Jem was a little puzzled by the urgency of the Irishman's voice. 'I reckon you can come tonight. If you want.'

'Tell your sister,' the man paused for a moment, his hand on his grimy forehead as though he were searching for forgotten words, 'tell her I'll be there tonight, and it's honoured and grateful I am for the chance of such fine lodgings.'

'What is this? What is this, please? A tea-party of the vicar? Teacups down, ladies; you have work to do.'

It was an amazing voice that had interrupted. A voice with a strong foreign accent. Jem turned round to stare, while all the navvies groaned exaggeratedly, and the sight that met his eyes was even more extraordinary than the voice. A one-legged man, his hair in a pigtail like an old-fashioned sailor's, was waving his crutch at them. His wooden right leg was painted brightly, like a barge, with flowers and people and houses. Jem gazed with his eyes wide. He had never seen such an exotic sight in all his life.

A sharp elbow caught him in the shoulder. Con was pushing him away and muttering. 'Pigtail. The ganger. Best be off with you.'

But Pigtail had already seen him. 'A boy?' His black eyes lit up and he ran his glance round the circle of navvies to make sure they were all watching him. 'A juicy and fat country boy.' His red tongue flicked over thin lips. 'Come here to me, country boy. I am feeling hungry.'

The foreign lilt of his voice and the evil glitter of his eye were too much for Jem. All at once, he found himself stumbling back down the cutting, as if he had seen a monster, while the loud laughter of the men pursued him. It wasn't that he *really* thought Pigtail would eat him, he told himself defiantly. But— He did not slow right down to a walk until his feet were on the familiar turf again, away from the strange, noisy world of the line. Only then did he glance back over his shoulder, ashamed to think of how he had run.

He sauntered back through the village, whistling carelessly, as though nothing had ever broken his composure. As he passed the bakehouse, the sound of Elijah Day's old mother croaking abuse at her son cheered him up a bit. 'Even Kate'd be not so bad. Not after that,' he thought. 'Could be I'll even get rid of her after all.' And the spring came back into his step.

When he got back to the cottage, he found Kate half-way across the floor, a bucket at her side and a scrubbing brush in her hand. Again.

'Wonder those bricks don't crumble right away.'

She took no notice. 'You seen him?'

'Yes.'

'And?'

'I said what you said.'

He sat down and began to take off his boots, enjoying his game. She rose to it beautifully, her face reddening as she fumed with impatience.

'Come on, boy!'

'Mmm?' He turned to her, all smiling innocence, and realized that the game was done. If he spun it out any

40

longer, he risked a cuff on the head. Quickly he nodded. 'He'll come. Tonight.'

'*Tonight?*' She bent over the floor and began to scrub twice as fast.

'He said,' Jem had suddenly remembered the exact message and he said the words with an imitation of Conor's serious politeness, to tease her, 'he said he was honoured and grateful for the chance of such fine lodgings.'

Kate stopped scrubbing for a moment. 'He's got a tongue on him, that one,' she said with elaborate unconcern. And then, with a careless movement, she sent the whole bucket of water flooding across the floor.

CHAPTER FOUR

Conor came at sunset, a black shape looming in the cottage doorway, his outline deformed by bundles. In one hand he carried his tools and some things wrapped up in a blue cloth, and in the other he held a battered leather bag which was crazily patched with scraps of carpet. He hovered awkwardly on the step, waiting for Kate to make the first move and invite him inside.

She attacked at once, graciously but firmly.

'Good evening to you, Mr O'Flynn. I like boots off at the door. Keeps the place cleaner.'

Conor glanced to one side and saw Jem's boots lined up neatly beside Kate's iron-soled pattens.

'Sure and I beg your pardon.' He stacked his belongings precariously on the mud by the door and, balancing in an ungainly way on first one leg and then the other, took off his one brown boot and his one black boot. Jem looked furiously at Kate. She knew very well that he never took off his boots until he was inside. But she was standing, arms folded, gazing watchfully at the Irishman. There was a hint of triumph in her eye as he lined his boots up tidily beside theirs. But he removed the triumph by saying, in a perfectly friendly fashion, 'You'll need to be reminding me of the ways of decent folk, for I've been too long up at the camp.'

As he dumped his bundles inside, Kate gave a noisy sigh at the muddy marks they made on the floor, but he did not seem to notice, being busy rummaging for something in his leather bag. Finding it, he brought it out with a flourish.

'There you are, Miss Penfold. Supper.'

Kate and Jem gaped unashamedly. It was a vast piece of salt beef, weighing five pounds or so, wrapped in a square of muslin. As the folds fell away and they could see the full splendour of it, they gasped.

'It's for all of us now,' said Conor anxiously. 'To share. Don't be taking it amiss.'

'We can't—' Kate began. Then she stopped and Jem could hear, as clearly as if she spoke them, the thoughts that struggled in her head. She was reluctant to be beholden to a rough, vulgar navvy. But here was a chance to feed them all properly in a way that rejoiced her housewifely heart and her hungry stomach. Slowly she reached out her hand.

'Thank you,' she said, in a voice quite different from the hectoring briskness with which she had greeted him. 'Thank you kindly, Mr O'Flynn.'

His face relaxed into a smile. 'Faith, it's nothing.' Bending down, he began to rummage again. 'I've a few things here I'd be glad of a place for on the dresser and about. Nothing much, you understand. Just a few bits and pieces.'

Jem could have laughed aloud at Kate's face as she swallowed the idea of having a navvy's knicknacks on her dresser. And how could she refuse, with his lump of salt beef in her hand? In ten minutes, Conor's clock was on the window-sill, his gaudy tin tray and his fairground mug with its leering, painted face were on the dresser. 'Dust-traps!' Kate muttered to Jem under her breath. But it was the only sign of her feelings that she allowed herself.

In twenty minutes, Conor had the whole room arranged to his taste, by dint of apologetic suggestions and offers of help, dandling the baby on his knee while Kate cooked and Jem worked in the garden.

When the meal had been eaten, the largest meal that

Kate and Jem could remember for years, Conor leaned backwards and loosened his belt. Lifting one of his stockinged feet and then the other, he thumped them down on to the table in front of him.

Kate coughed.

'Got trouble with your chest, have you?' the Irishman asked blithely. 'Isn't that bad luck now? A bonny girl like you.'

'Your feet, Mr O'Flynn,' Kate said coldly.

He looked at them, wiggling one of his big toes through a hole in his sock. Jem saw Kate press her lips firmly together.

'Your feet, Mr O'Flynn,' she said again. 'They're on the table.'

'Bless me now!' He stared at them as if they had jumped up there by themselves. 'So they are, to be sure. Will I take them off?'

'Please.'

With a grin that spread half across his face, the Irishman lifted them down, one after the other. 'I can see you'll be keeping me in order while I stop here, Miss Penfold. I'll have to forget my navvy manners for sure.'

Jem chuckled softly. He could see that Conor was teasing Kate, trying to get her to soften and join in the joke of having a rough navvy sitting at her table waiting to be tamed. But Kate did not see the joke. She gave a brisk, businesslike nod.

'I like to keep a nice house.'

Conor looked at her with a strange, unexpected gentleness. 'And it's like I've told you. I've fallen out of Christian ways in the life I've been leading. But I'll learn them again from you.'

There was a soft, unnerving pause. For some reason, the blood rushed into Kate's face and she looked down at her plate, pushing a piece of bread around with her finger.

Just as the silence began to grow difficult, Conor gave a quick shout of laughter and levered himself out of his chair.

'Well now, if I'm to be learning how Christian men live in this village you'll have to be telling me what they do when they've had their dinners. Do they take a turn round the green for a pint of beer, maybe?'

'No,' said Kate quickly. Almost rudely.

To soften it, Jem added, 'There's no inn in the village. And not the money for drinking.'

'They sit indoors then?' Con scratched his head. 'No getting together for a bit of a chat?'

'Oh, they do,' said Jem. 'At the forge. There's always some of them down there of an evening. Nothing much else to do.'

'Well then, let's be taking a turn down there.' Con rammed his old hat on to his head and began to pull on his boots.

'But you can't—' Kate looked up quickly.

'And why not?' said the Irishman. 'Wouldn't I want to be meeting my neighbours now? Getting a bit friendly with them?'

'But they won't—' started Kate. Then she looked steadily at him. He was standing in the doorway waiting for Jem, a calm, solid man with a smile on his lips.

'A person should be friendly with his neighbours,' he said quietly. 'And it's only a fool who would sit indoors waiting for others to come to him. It's my part to go to them and hold out my hand. Are you coming, Jem?'

Slowly, not quite understanding, Jem put on his boots and Kate shrugged and started to push the plates together jerkily. 'Go on then,' she said. 'Go on. You'll see.'

'We'll not be long,' said Con. 'Come on, Jem.'

The two of them tramped down the garden path silently. As they went through the gate, Conor clapped Jem on the shoulder. 'Which way then, lad? Up the village is it?'

'This way,' Jem said.

'Fine. We'll just go up and have a bit of a chat for an hour or so.'

'They might not . . . ' Jem looked up at the big man beside him. 'I mean . . . if they know you're a navvy—'

'Look, lad, what else can I do? Should I spend my time skulking in your cottage because I haven't the spirit to try my luck? Are they such fearsome men in this village of yours that they'll eat me?'

At once Jem felt easier, knowing that Conor understood. After all, he was right. What could the men do? Jem grinned in the dark. 'Some of them will do anything for a good meal.'

'Good luck to them.' Conor chuckled. 'I've a tin of salt in my pocket if they fancy a bit of savour to their meat. Is this the place now?'

Jem looked towards the half-open door of the forge. He could see a dozen figures, lit a dull red by the dying fire, and his ears, straining to catch the tone of the voices inside, heard only a tired, amiable muttering, with none of the smith's loud ranting. Tonight was a quiet night. Encouraged, he stepped through the door into the warmth. The smith saw him at once.

'It's young Jem!' he bellowed, noisy but friendly. 'That sister of yours has let you out, has she? Thought she'd be needing you at home to protect her. I hear you've been having a visit from Mrs Neville.'

The men round the fire roared with laughter, but Joe Hamage had already caught sight of the other figure standing outside in the dark.

46

'Step farther in, lad,' he said. 'There's someone else behind you waiting to get in. Is it old Hoppy?'

'No, it's—' Jem stopped and stood to one side to let Conor come in. He walked in as calm as ever and nodded round at the men.

'Good evening to you all.'

Jem saw them straighten uneasily as they heard the Irish in his voice, but no one spoke for a moment. They stared at Conor, taking in his confident bearing, his unmistakable navvy clothes, a world away from the old embroidered smocks that most of the men wore.

'Well now,' said the smith at last, slowly rubbing his chin, 'who's this you've brought with you, young Jem?'

'It's—' Jem gulped. 'It's our lodger, Mr O'Flynn.'

'And I'm pleased to meet you all,' Conor said, smiling round again.

But no one smiled back. They were watching the smith to see what he would do next. And the smith went on staring at Jem.

'Tell us then,' he said softly at last, 'where have you been to be finding a lodger like that?'

'He's from—' started Jem, but the smith suddenly shouted, interrupting him.

'We know where he's from. No need to tell us. We *know*!'

'That's right, then,' Conor said easily. 'I'm a bold, bad navvy from up by the line.'

His imperturbable humour almost worked. One or two of the men sniggered, not unkindly. It would have been hard to imagine anyone looking less bold and bad than Conor did at that moment. He had tilted his battered felt hat backwards on his head and ruffled up the front of his hair, making himself look almost foolish. Jem sensed a faint loosening in the atmosphere, as if the

47

men were finding a navvy at close quarters more human than they had expected. Conor held out his hand.

'Conor O'Flynn's my name. Kilkenny Con, they call me.'

One of the nearest men actually moved forward, as if to take the outstretched hand, but the smith looked at him coldly and spoke again.

'And what, *Mister* O'Flynn, brings you to my forge?'

'Well, sure, I've come to say good evening to my new neighbours.'

The smith took a step nearer the fire, so that he faced Conor across the red embers. Coming from below, the light sent devilish shadows up his massive face, curving his eyebrows upwards.

'We're no neighbours of yours,' he said.

It was as if every man in the forge held his breath. A close, tense silence. The men knew that the smith's words were meant as a challenge and they waited to see whether the Irishman would take it up. But Conor ignored the smith's tone of voice.

'Faith,' he said lightly, 'a man like me must take his neighbours where he finds them.'

'Not in my forge.' The smith moved round the fire slightly, so that there was nothing between the two of them but a yard of empty space. 'Get out. We don't want the likes of you in this village.'

Conor lowered the hand he had held out all this time. 'How would you know what sort I am, then? Without taking the trouble to speak to me?'

Joe Hamage's great hands clenched into fists. 'Are you going to leave?'

For a moment, Jem was certain that there would be a fight. He saw Conor's fingers curl into his palm, waited for them to tense and slam out at the smith. It made a queer kind of sense. A good straight fight. If he won, the men would respect him. Might even make a place for him. They were all leaning forward expectantly to see what kind of stuff the newcomer was made of. Half-curled, Conor's fingers hovered briefly. Then, one by one, they straightened out and his hands dropped to his sides.

'Well now.' He looked round at them all. 'I'm not a man to be staying where I'm not wanted. Good night to you all.'

He turned quickly and strode out of the forge and the men let out their held breath with a low, jeering sound. Joe Hamage's face loosened into a triumphant sneer as he looked towards Jem.

'A proper weak-stomached one you've got there, boy. I thought navvies were supposed to be brave as lions.'

Unable to speak, Jem stumbled out after Conor, hearing the tension behind him break into loud, relieved laughter. He could see the navvy's tall figure ahead of him in the dark, but his disappointment was so strong that he walked slowly on purpose, so that he did not catch up until Conor stopped for him.

The Irishman put a hand on the boy's shoulder. 'What's up with you then, lad?'

'They thought—' horrified, Jem heard himself choke on the words—'they thought you were afraid.'

'Well now,' Conor sounded almost amused, 'and that could have been the truth, couldn't it? What do you think?'

Jem called the scene back into his mind, remembering how Con had stood steady in the red firelight. 'Not afraid. But you should have fought him.'

'And for what? Would that have answered all their anger about the navvies? To be rolling round in the dust like a pair of senseless boys?'

49

Jem frowned and then burst out, 'But they thought you were afraid. They thought you were a *coward*!'

'And what harm is that to me?' said Conor. 'I'm the only one to know the truth of that and I know I wasn't afraid.' He paused a moment with his hand on the front gate. '*I* wasn't afraid, but it could be that they were.'

That made no kind of sense to Jem at all. Why would a crowd of men be afraid of one navvy who would not fight? Impatiently, he pushed through the gate and went first into the cottage. Kate was sitting by the fireside in the half-dark, with the baby on her knee.

'Back already?' she said, without looking round. 'That was a short visit.' As Conor shut the front door of the cottage, she peered over her shoulder at him. 'How did you find Joe Hamage?'

'He'd be the big man?' Conor looked at Jem, who nodded. 'A fine figure of a man he is. Sure, he fancied roasting me over the fire and making his supper off me.'

Kate snorted. 'A child could have told you the way it would be.'

'Give them time,' the Irishman said. 'Folk like those need a deal of time to be growing used to incomers.'

'Time!' Kate said scornfully. Getting up, she shifted the baby to her hip and went across to the front door. Without saying anything, she began to struggle with the heavy bolt, but it was stiff, because they hardly ever used it, and she could not move it one-handed. Conor went over and did it for her and the three of them looked at the iron rod shutting up the door. Then Kate said, 'More time than you've got, maybe. You'd best be treading carefully while you stop in this village, Mr O'Flynn.'

'Like a spring lamb I'll be. Now, if you'll show me where my bed is I'll be off to sleep.'

Kate told him, briefly, and she and Jem listened to his stockinged feet padding up the narrow staircase. Then Kate said, 'There's a man who doesn't know when he's come back lucky. I was waiting to hear that Joe had broken all his teeth.'

'He wouldn't fight,' Jem said dully. 'He told me he couldn't see the sense in it.'

It was impossible to tell whether Kate was pleased at that. All she said was, 'Could be he's learned his lesson without. Perhaps now we'll not be hearing any more of this nonsense about mixing with the village.'

But, as Jem went upstairs to bed, he was remembering how Joe and Conor had faced each other across the fire, how the village men had waited for something to happen. And he could not agree with Kate that that was the end of it. Between Joe and Conor, between the village and the navvies, there was a quarrel started. Somewhere, some time, it would be picked up again.

CHAPTER FIVE

The next evening, after supper, Kate looked challengingly at Conor as she cleared the plates away.

'Well, Mr O'Flynn? Ready to look for some village men to talk to?'

'Oh now.' Con pretended to look disappointed. 'And there was I thinking you would be wanting me to stay in and talk to you.'

Kate said nothing. She just gave a tight, satisfied smile and finished clearing the table. But Jem, given the chance, began to quiz Conor about the line. His questions went on and on.

' . . . and the ganger. What's he? A right queer voice he had.'

'Pigtail?' Conor leaned back, his eyes narrowed in admiration. 'There's a man for you now.'

'Foreign is he? From somewhere up country?'

Conor chuckled. 'Indeed, that's your own countrymen you're talking of, lad. No, Pigtail's none of those. A proper *foreign* foreigner is Pigtail. Wandering Spanish, like no man I've ever met before. There's no knowing where he caught the trick of speaking English, but he was a sailor, a labourer, a common navvy and a tinker before he came to being a ganger. The tale of his life would be a fine thing to hear.'

'Is he—' Jem changed what he had been going to say. 'You like him?'

But Conor knew what had been in his head, and he laughed softly, in puffs through his nose. 'Put the fear of God into you, did he? Well, now, I've never *heard* that he ate boys . . .'

'Course not,' Jem said quickly, his face red. 'Thought he was fierce, that's all.'

'And you're not wrong there, boy. A bad man to have against you in a quarrel is Pigtail. There's never a man can make him flinch, for he cares for nothing but the work and the money. But a good man to work under if you've no fear of sweat.'

'But queer,' Jem said musingly and, as he had hoped, his half-questioning set the Irishman off on a long run of stories about Pigtail's exploits, each wilder and more unbelievable than the last.

Kate sat silent on the other side of the hearth, her needle catching the glow from the fire and her eyes straining at the stitches in the light of the single candle. It did not seem that she was listening, but every now and then she gave a low cough and, whenever she did, Conor would look up at her quickly and change the drift of his story. Each time, Jem gritted his teeth, furious at being protected like a child, but it was not worth making a fuss. There was too much to hear and too little time to hear it all.

And so, from day to day, it went on. Conor seemed content to come back to the cottage of an evening and sit chatting to Jem while Kate sewed Mrs Neville's linen. It was as though he had really made the place his home. Signs of his presence multiplied, in the house and in the garden, as he set his hand to tasks that had gone undone before he came. The hedge was tidied and pruned and the weak catch on the staircase door was mended. He fixed shelves in the scullery and put the broken stool together again.

But the plainest sign of his stay with them was the top shelf of the dresser. He had a strange habit, when he paid his rent each week, of bringing Kate a present, and he chose to bring her little jugs, such as the other cottage women loved to collect when they had a few pennies to spare for fairings. Blue-striped, or painted with violets, or labelled 'A Present from Helmston', they warmed and brightened the drab little cottage with their colours. Kate murmured sharply while she dusted them, but Jem noticed that she had begun to make a rag rug for the hearth in the little time she had to spare.

Without realizing it, Jem was separating himself from the village. A distance was coming between him and the village people, who had refused to take Conor's hand, as though he and Kate and Conor, cosy in the firelight, were the only real people. His days were spent crow-keeping, alone in the new-sown fields, and every evening he stayed at home listening to Conor instead of going down to the forge. But it did not occur to him how long it was since he had seen Ben until there were five jugs on the dresser and he met Ben one day in the lane. His friend crossed to the other side and made as if to go by with his eyes cast down.

'Here! Ben!'

'Yes? Oh,' Ben tried to look surprised, 'it's you.' He always had been a bad liar.

'Course it's me. What's your game walking past like that?'

A vague expression came into Ben's voice, but his round, freckled face, more honest than he wished, showed how hurt he was. 'I thought—happen you'd no time for old friends.'

'Aw, don't talk daft.'

'With your navvy mates and all.'

Jem could have punched him. 'Here, don't be a ninny. I'll come up the forge tonight. If I'm welcome to come, that is.' He watched Ben carefully, trying to see where he stood, but his friend just shrugged casually.

'Don't do us any favours. It's up to you.'

It was a dare, and Jem knew it. 'None of that. Course I want to come,' he insisted, all the more strongly because he did not really want to. 'Honest. I've had a sight too much to do these last weeks, that's all.' He tried to push Ben into cheerfulness. 'You know. Kate.'

Ben met his eyes and gave him a weak grin. 'Time she was wed.' But it was without the old bounce, as though he had no heart for the joke. Jem gave him a friendly push.

'I'll bet you they're just waiting on old Mrs Day to die.' But it was no use. Ben was ready to be friendly now, but not ready to laugh. Inwardly, Jem shrugged it off. Time enough.

'See you tonight then. When I've had my tea.'

'Likely.' With a wave of his hand behind him, Ben was away, leaving Jem to plod on home.

He felt as though the last thing he wanted was to drag out again that evening. After a day of running up and down the ploughed slopes of Little Piece, shaking the heavy crow-rattle and shouting, he ached in every inch and longed for his bed.

But by the time he had finished his meal he was glad of the excuse to go out. Kate was in a rare temper, for no reason that he could see, banging round the cottage and snarling at him every time he moved, and Conor, for once, had not come back, so that there was no one to soften the edge of Kate's anger. Jem caught it all. He stood it for half an hour and then trailed down to the forge, more willingly than he had expected.

As soon as he got there, he knew that something was wrong. The murmur that came from the forge was not the single bellow of Ben's father, nor the lazy, intermittent drone of the other men, but a steady low humming, fast and urgent like bees set to attack. Jem peered round the door and saw the fire banked high and the men pressed in, shoulder tight to shoulder, more than forty of them crammed into the little forge. Nearly all the men in the village, except for Elijah Day, whose mother never let him down the forge.

Ben was over the far side, trapped by the crush of bodies. As his eyes met Jem's, he gave a sympathetic grimace, gesturing his helplessness. At the same moment, the smith saw Jem and let out a roar.

'Well, well, the little navvy. What do you want, boy?'

Jem stuck up his chin bravely. 'I came for Ben.'

A shout of scornful laughter came from the smith, filling the forge.

'Found half a minute for old mates, have you?' His face fell into nasty lines and his voice menaced. 'We don't want any navvy-lovers here. Get yourself off.'

The fear in Jem's knees made them tremble, but he stood his ground. 'Who're you calling a navvy-lover?'

'So you don't like it?' Joe's voice dropped to a dangerous gentleness. 'Over here, boy.' And he beckoned with a thick, dirty finger. 'By the fire. Where I can get a proper sight of you.'

As Jem pushed his way between the other men, they were silent, drawing back from him in a strange way and watching Joe uncertainly, to see if he was set to explode in one of his black rages. None of them looked at Jem and even Ben only smiled hesitantly. Coming into the centre of the group, Jem looked round at the faces, so familiar and so cold, and planted himself foursquare to the smith.

'Here I am.' His voice sounded high and thin in the stuffy air.

'There you are.' The blacksmith's hand fell heavy on his shoulder. 'Still one of us, then, are you?'

'Course.' Jem's eyes flicked round the circle again, and men he had known all his life avoided them.

'Well then,' Joe put a rough finger under the boy's chin, tilting it painfully upward to look him in the eye, 'talk.'

Jem was silent, not knowing what he could say, and after a pause the smith went on softly, 'How many of them up the line?'

'About a thousand, Con says.' Jem swallowed the lump in his throat, but it did not go away.

'All Papists and Irish?'

'Not all. Mostly.' He could feel the hair on the back of his neck prickle, and the air of the forge quivered with danger.

'We're tired.' Joe's voice began to grow louder. He was talking to them all now, his words swelling out. 'Tired of that Irish scum around us, insulting our women and randying through our villages. They got paid today. Broke up the pub at Little Morden and poured beer on George Fuller. Must we stand for it? Must we?'

He shook Jem roughly by the shoulder as he repeated the question, and then lowered his face to within an inch or two of Jem's, so that Jem could see the marks on his yellow teeth and smell the stink of his breath.

'What'll we do, lad?' His fingers dug deeper into the boy's shoulder.

'Fight,' stuttered Jem foolishly, his teeth banging together. With one voice, the men let out a bitter laugh, and the smith's fingers squeezed and kneaded.

'Try again, boy. Forty of us can't take on a thousand. Not even a thousand Irish. Try again.'

His eyes gleamed with pleasure at the game he was playing with the boy, relishing the fear and pain in his face. Jem looked quickly from side to side. The other men were gazing down at the floor, embarrassed. Ben met his eyes sympathetically for a moment and then he, too, glanced away.

'Come on.' The fingers were like iron and the pain cleared Jem's mind briefly.

'*You* fight. Just one of them. A challenge, like.'

The grip on his shoulder loosened and a queer, almost flattered expression spread over Joe's face. When Jem could think again, he realized that the pain had made him wise. The smith was wrestling champion of all the villages for miles around. None but Jem's father had challenged him these ten years. The random suggestion had touched the nerve of his vanity, and murmurs of relieved approval came from the other men.

'That's it, for sure. Our man and theirs.'

'We'll show them.'

'Yes. A challenge, Joe, a challenge.'

They clamoured like children in school. It was a gesture they could make, a way they could hold their own against the incomers.

Joe addressed them, with majestic dignity. 'Well, lads, what's it to be? A challenge?'

'YES!' they answered in a single shout, and the blacksmith turned back to Jem.

'That lodger of yours. He'll take the challenge?'

'Yes. Likely.'

'Well, tell him—' Joe searched his mind for the details. 'Tell him to say I'll be up back of the Copse at four in the afternoon, Sunday's a week. And I'll wrestle any man they send.'

'Right.' With the speed of relief, Jem turned to wriggle back through the press, but the smith caught at his smock.

'Not so fast, my lad.' Clearly he was minded to carry on his game a little longer. 'You'll be up at the wrestling? And cheering?'

'Happen.' Jem turned slowly to look at him.

The question rapped out sharply across the forge. 'Who for?'

Jem had not even thought about it, but now there was only one answer he could give. 'You.'

'I'll be listening,' the smith crooned evilly, holding Jem with his eye as a fox holds a rabbit.

'Best let the lad go, Joe.' Hoppy Noyce's calm voice came to break the spell and Jem pushed through the crowd and shot out of the door, a roar of laughter following at his heels. His eyes prickled with tears of humiliation and he ran on through the village, filled with a grinding rage, as he wished that he were old enough to fight the smith himself, and hit him and hit him and hit him—

He raced in at the door of the cottage and slammed it behind him, leaning back on it while he panted, as if he were being chased. Kate, still stitching in the half-light of the fire, looked up and snapped, 'Bee stung you?'

'It's nothing,' he said automatically. Second nature now to keep things from her. As he flopped on to a stool and began unlacing his boots, he looked around.

'Con still out?'

She shrugged sourly.

'Where is he?'

'Best not ask.' She sniffed. 'But I doubt it's any use sitting up. Off to bed.'

'But I've a message to him.'

'What must wait has to keep.' Then it got through to her. 'What message?'

'Nothing.'

'You—'

But whatever she had been going to say was lost in a sudden burst of song from the gate. She jumped to her feet and stared at the door, white-faced and trembling with rage. '*Him!* Foul and drunk!'

As Conor came through the door, she stepped in front of him, a slight figure, rigid with fury. 'Stop it this *minute*! Stop it!'

The shock of it stopped him at once, and he looked in blank puzzlement from one Penfold to another. But before he could speak Kate started up again.

'This is a decent house. How *dare* you come in drunk? I've heard tell of your paydays, and your doings up at Little Morden. Disgusting, it is! You'll pack your bags and leave in the morning!'

Then she stared at him wide-eyed, almost afraid of what she had said and of her own wildness. Conor waited, to be sure she was quite finished, and then he spoke.

'It's your house, Miss Penfold, and I'm ready to do whatever you say. But you'd best remember it's not only drunken men that sing. Goodnight to you.'

With massive, quiet dignity he walked to the stairs, and they could hear his feet climbing them steadily, without a stumble. Kate's mouth was half-open, as though she would have called back her words and to Jem, shaken and bruised, the incident was the last straw. He hissed furiously at her, 'A fair fool you've made of yourself! You're a sour old maid, without a kind word in you for anyone.'

She brushed her hand over her eyes, coming back to herself. 'Happen I was a bit hasty. In the morning—' Then she shook herself back to briskness. 'Off to bed with you. Give over gaping at me.'

Conor was a black hill in the bed, his back turned, when Jem climbed in, but his breathing gave him away and, after listening for a moment, Jem whispered, 'Conor?'

'Yes?' It was barely audible.

'I've a message for you. From the village men.'

'For me?' The black shape heaved over to face him. 'And what would they be wanting with me, now?'

'There's to be a fight. With Joe Hamage.'

'The smith?' Conor yawned. 'A fine man for a fight. Good luck to him.'

'No, wait—' for the navvy showed signs of rolling back—'that's not it. It's a message to the navvies, them up at the camp. A challenge.' He began to gabble the words as near as he could to what Joe had said. 'One of you to wrestle him. Up back of the Copse, Sunday's a week at four o'clock.'

'That's grand.' Conor's voice was not so sleepy now. 'Tell him we'll be sending him a man can beat him into the hillside with one fist. If they *will* have it that way.'

He sounded almost cheerful, and Jem tried to find some way of telling him that it was not a game, but all he could say was, 'He's a big man. And fair angry.'

Conor laughed quietly as he turned over to sleep. 'Sure and isn't it only a bit of fun? A smith and a navvy. A fine match.'

Jem stared at the steep black shape of Con's back and suddenly burst out again.

'Conor?'

'Mmmmm?' It was good-humoured, but almost asleep.

'Are you drunk?'

A soft, rueful chuckle answered him. 'Five pints of beer. Maybe six. That's drinking, you'll allow. But a drunken navvy drinks pints of *gin*, lad.'

'Then why did Kate—?'

'Folk see what they think to see,' Conor said a little sadly. 'Especially decent folk. Now be off to sleep.'

But Jem had one more thing to say first.

'Kate said—'

'Mmmmm?'

'She said you could stay.' Well, and so she had. Almost. 'Will you?'

Unruffled, Conor murmured, 'And isn't there the pig to kill on Thursday? Why would I want to be leaving?'

Jem curled to sleep on his own side of the bed, smiling.

Chapter Six

Pigsticking. The thought of it leapt into Jem's mind when he woke next morning, flooding it with pictures as he remembered last year. His father, tall and laughing, scraping the pig with a group of village men who joked and helped. His mother, serving up bread and beer to everyone and tossing potato cakes to the children who played round the wash-house. And the pig feast the next Sunday, with all their friends from the village, who always shared it because the Penfolds had no near kin. Jem sighed inwardly as he swung his legs out of bed. Things had changed since last year. But still his heart stirred and his mouth watered. After all, a pigsticking was still a pigsticking. It was enough to send all thoughts of the fight to the back of his head. Enough also, apparently, to make Kate forget what she had said to Conor, for there was no more talk of his leaving.

On the Saturday morning before the pigsticking, Kate looked up at Jem as she ladled out his water gruel for breakfast. 'You off work today?'

'Yes. Till Wednesday, likely.'

'Well, if I'm to have you hanging round the house you'd best make yourself useful. Take yourself up to the bakehouse and tell Mr Day we're killing the pig Thursday, and would he kindly come down after second bake.'

Jem had run this errand many times in the past, for Elijah Day had always been pig-killer as well as baker, but this was the first time that Kate had sent him. He tried to raise a chuckle at the message. Kate and Elijah Day. Only, somehow, it did not seem so funny without

Ben to share the joke. He gulped his breakfast and set off up the lane.

As he came into the Days' yard, the thick, yeasty air from the bake filled his nostrils and he knew that Elijah would be taking a rest until the batch was cooked, so he went past the open bakehouse door and knocked at the door of the kitchen, on the other side of the yard.

'Come.'

Elijah sat at the table, a shapeless mound of pale flesh, topped by straggling, greasy curls. In one hand he held an outsize mug of tea and in the other a wedge of lardy cake, black with currants and glistening with fat and sugar. Jem could almost taste the heavy sweetness, but he knew it was no good staring. Elijah would never give you a bit. Anyway, at that moment he looked far from pleased to see Jem.

'Oh . . . er . . . Jem Penfold. Er . . . what can I—'

'Who is it, then?' His mother's scream, from upstairs, cut him short, but he took no other notice of it. He watched Jem.

'Please, Mr Day, Kate says we're killing the pig Thursday and would you come up after second bake?'

'Well . . . er . . . I—' Elijah looked sheepish and plunged his teeth back into the lardy cake.

'E*l*ijah! Have I got to come down?'

Jem waited. After a pause, Elijah put down the lardy cake, chewed, swallowed.

'I . . . er . . . I don't rightly know. Not about that.'

'You won't?' Jem stared at him incredulously. 'Not kill our pig?'

'EL-I-JAH! Drat the boy!' Mutterings and thumps came down the stairs, and old Mrs Day stormed into the kitchen, her walking-stick impatient on the tiles. When she saw Jem and Elijah staring silently at each other, she twitched and thumped.

'Jem Penfold. What do you want, boy? Eh?'

Jem stepped back slightly. He had always been scared of old Mrs Day.

'I came to tell Mr Day we're killing the pig Thursday, but he—'

'Bread's done,' murmured Elijah, rising hastily to his feet and wobbling his way across the kitchen and out over the yard. Mrs Day looked shrewdly at Jem.

'He being funny? Eh?'

'Well,' Jem looked down. 'Seems like he won't come.'

She sighed noisily, casting her eyes up to the ceiling.

'The man's a fool. An utter fool. Let me at him. Stay here, boy.'

Twitch and thump across the yard. Through the doorway of the bakehouse, Jem could see the two of them talking. At least, old Mrs Day was talking, waving her hand about and stepping back every now and then to avoid the hot tins that Elijah was shovelling out of the chest-high oven. He worked steadily with the long peel, seeming never to pause in his pattern of sliding the flat end in empty and bringing it out loaded with tins, apparently saying nothing. Yet, when the oven was empty and he put down the peel and started to pull on the sacking mittens, so that he could tip the bread out of the tins, Mrs Day came back across the yard.

'That's all right then, boy. He'll be there.'

'But is he—?'

'Ask no questions.' She ushered Jem briskly towards the door and then, as though she had made up her mind about something, she went on speaking with a jerk. 'You can tell that sister of yours from me that she's got a good, sensible head on her. And that all the men in the village are stupid fools.' With a nod and another twitch, she turned back to the table and cut a big wedge of lardy cake, which she thrust into Jem's hand as she pushed him out of the door. He wandered home thoughtfully, munching. Elijah's behaviour seemed to make no sense.

But it made a lot of sense by the end of the day. The rest of Jem's task for the day was to knock on every door in the village, announcing the pigsticking and asking for help, and by the time he had knocked on three or four doors he began to realize how much things had changed since last year. At every door, he met blank stares, faces turned away in embarrassment, sometimes even anger. Gradually it dawned on him that no one was going to come.

Not even Hoppy Noyce. Hoppy's cottage was nearly at the end of the village and as Jem came to it, feeling bruised inside, he allowed himself a small quiver of hope. He tapped gently, praying that Hoppy had come home to his lunch.

That wish, at least, was granted. Hoppy opened the door, a bit of bread in one hand, and gave him a small smile.

'Hallo, Jem lad. What's up?'

'Our pigsticking, Mr Noyce. Thursday after second bake. Can you—' But his voice petered out. Hoppy was already shaking his head sadly.

'Can't be done, lad. If it was only me, perhaps I'd take a chance. You know me. I'm not one to be at odds with anyone. But there's her in there. She'd carry on something terrible.'

'You'll not come?' Jem could hear his voice cracking.

'I'm sorry, lad. 'Twouldn't be fair.'

Hoppy's embarrassment was as great as Jem's, the old face crinkled with worry. But he did not change what he had said.

'Makes no odds,' mumbled Jem gruffly, turning away and stumbling straight back to his own cottage. He had no heart now for knocking on the last few doors. He could not hope that anything different would happen there. All the village had turned away from him. Nearly all the people he knew. He sat at his tea, chewing morosely, not even aware that Conor had brought home a large lump of bacon to share with them. It might have been anything in his mouth. At last he burst out, without explanation, 'Why? What've we done?'

Kate shrugged and Con looked down into his plate.

'Kate?' Jem pursued. She had made no reply when he had told her. Now he was determined to get one.

'For the love of heaven,' she said impatiently, 'don't be more of a fool than God made you.'

'Con? You mean it's all because of Con?'

And then he saw, as Con pushed away his plate and went to sit by the fire, that he had not been tactful. Kate kicked him painfully under the table, and he almost shouted, overcome by the injustice of it all.

'If they're so cross, why don't they go up the line and get taken on themselves?'

Kate was silent and he looked at Con, busy filling his pipe.

'There's some would be glad of it, lad, but it's not everyone the gangers fancy taking on,' the Irishman said quietly. 'There's no shortage of men. Two there were got turned away yesterday.'

Jem went back to his meal, muttering, longing to kick the table and fling the food across the room. But he knew there would be no more if he did. As he finished, Con's voice came rather apologetically from the fireplace.

'There's others would happily come to help with the pig. If you should want them.'

'Is that so?' The wariness in Kate's voice showed that she knew what he was going to say.

'My mates from up the line. One of them would come and glad to. If you want.'

Serve the village right, Jem thought, still bitter. Serve them right if we fill our house with navvies and break up the village once a week. What have we *done*?

Kate was clattering the dishes together and clearing the table. When she got to the scullery door she turned.

'Thank you, Mr O'Flynn,' she said stiffly. 'It's a good idea.' And she went through.

Looking at Con, Jem was surprised to see the slow, rich smile which spread over his face.

Kate shot out of bed on Thursday morning and began to scrub and sweep as though a thousand villagers were coming to the pigsticking instead of two navvies and a reluctant baker. Jem watched her, as he stood outside the back door chopping wood for the copper.

'Got grand folks coming?'

'You shut your mouth, Jem Penfold. I keep a clean house whoever comes.' And she slammed the back door in his face and went on with her scrubbing.

Come eleven o'clock, everything was ready, the baby scrubbed pink and put to bed, the copper in the wash-house full of water, the wood stacked neatly underneath. Kate took Conor out to inspect the arrangements as she went to light the fire.

'You'll be scalding the creature and scraping it, then,' he said. 'Sure and isn't that heavy on the lifting? Back where I come from, we singe the bristles.'

'We scald,' Kate said firmly, as though change were impossible. 'Jem, run down to the bakehouse and ask Mr Day for the loan of his trestle. He should be next to ready by now.'

But Elijah was far from ready. Jem could see, as he got to the bakehouse, that the second bake was not even in the oven. The fat baker stood at the bins kneading round loaves against each other. Two lumps of pale dough and himself like a third. As Jem gave his message, Mrs Day came hurrying across the yard.

'Ten minutes he'll be. No more.'

'But the bake?'

'Tut, boy! Think I can't handle a peel any more? I'll send him up as soon as the bread's in the oven. Never fear. Take the bench with you, now.'

When Jem got back, he could see an unusual figure at the door of the wash-house. It was Ginger, swaggering about, clearly having come to help. Kate stood a little apart, trying not to hear the jokes that he was exchanging with Con, but not looking unfriendly.

'Hallo, young shaver. Remember me?'

'Hallo.' Jem was glad it was Ginger. He had been a little afraid it might be Pigtail.

'How long?' broke in Kate, glancing out into the lane.

'Ten minutes no more. That's what Mrs Day said.'

'Well, give us the bench then.' Conor held out a hand. 'We'll be tying the creature down, then, for he'll be here before we're done.'

Ginger and Con got the trestle placed to their liking inside the wash-house, and then began the game of catching the pig. Almost as though it guessed what was to come to it, it slid between their legs and ran round the garden, squealing with hunger and fear. At last it was caught and roped securely to the bench, but Elijah was long in coming and they had to listen to the pig squealing for five minutes or more before he turned in at the gate with his pigsticking-knife. The squeals had made all of them, except Ginger, restless and eager to get the business over, yet as Elijah stood looking down at the pig Jem wondered for a moment how he could do it. The two of them looked so like each other, fat and pale with small eyes. Like killing your brother it must be, Jem thought, and he felt a shiver draw him back from Elijah.

But, almost at once, he had to admit that the baker was good at this job. The pig was cleanly killed, the blood caught in a basin for black pudding, the carcass dumped into the copper to scald in the hot water. All with no fuss and hardly any noise.

Then they could all breathe easy. It was not their pig any more. It was a lump of meat covered in bristles which must be scraped off. Kate brought out the old pewter candlesticks they always used and Con, Elijah, and Ginger began on the task.

Scraping was raw work. They all took turns, Con and Elijah bearing the brunt of it, as being the most experienced, and their hands all grew pink and sore. Ginger complained all the time, with a wide grin on his face.

'Ruin my hands, this will. Ever heard of a navvy with washerwoman's hands? Take me a month to get them hard again.'

His bright flow of talk disguised the fact that Elijah was not speaking at all. He worked stolidly and silently, his little black eyes fixed on the pig, his arms immersed up to the elbows. Jem tried to have, by himself, the fun he would have had with Ben, watching for looks between Kate and Elijah, but he could not do it. Kate seemed almost pleasant today, beside Elijah.

The scraping took a lot of hard work, with repeated lifting and turning of the heavy carcass, and even with all of them at it it was a long job. Kate had to go off in the middle to feed the baby. But at last it was done and the pig was heaved up for the last time, to hang suspended from the ceiling hook. It swung there crazily, spinning slightly, and Elijah sharpened his knife again. Then, with a quick flick, he sliced it open so that the tripes came slithering out, to be caught and sorted.

Jem looked away. That slithery moment always turned his stomach. But he saw Elijah's face light up. Saw him almost lick his lips.

'Would you . . . er. . . . the cutting up . . . er—'

'Oh, be gone will you, man,' Con said impatiently. 'Didn't I learn the trick of cutting up a pig when I was a lad of twelve?'

To be gone was plainly what Elijah had wanted. Muttering 'Good day . . . er—' he packed up in a trice, gathered together half the innards, as the pig-killer's share, and was off up the lane before anyone could even say goodbye. The two navvies and the two Penfolds stared at each other.

'Queer 'un,' commented Ginger. But he sounded unsurprised, as though he had expected to find the village full of queer 'uns.

He spoke his mind more clearly when they were all finally settled round the fire. Kate had cooked them a feast of pig's fry and they made a placid party as they sat, full up and drowsy. Kate, unusually for her, nursed the sleeping baby, while Conor moved his fingers over the penny whistle, keeping it in his lap as if he were not yet ready to play it. Jem waited eagerly for more stories from the Irishman, but it was Ginger who spoke, leaning back happily and patting his stomach.

'A fine drop of grub, that. P'raps you're not so daft after all, Kilkenny.'

Con smiled, but said nothing, and Ginger rambled amiably on. 'Thought you were round the twist when you said you were coming down here to live. Among a load of crabby villagers.' He stopped abruptly and bobbed his head awkwardly at Kate. 'Beg your pardon, miss, but you know how it is as well as I do. They don't care for us navvies, village folks don't.' He turned back to the Irishman. 'Come on now, Con. Give it to us

71

straight. What's your caper? Never thought you would turn too finickety for the camp.'

Con said briefly, without looking up, 'I'd a fancy to save my money. A fine chance I'd have stood up at the camp, wouldn't I now? With beer everywhere and the food a price to make your hair drop out.'

It was a half-joking answer, clearly meant to turn away the question, and Ginger fell back into silence. But Kate asked suddenly, 'What for? What are you saving your money for?'

Conor thought gravely for a moment, as though he must give her a proper answer, and then, looking her straight in the eye, he began slowly to explain.

'Well, it's ten years now I've been a navvy. Ten hard years and grand ones. But I'm coming on to thirty now and there's times the wish to be back in Kilkenny gets me so that I can hardly keep from running for the boat. But it's a hard land for a man that has nothing.' He paused, shaking his head slowly, as though remembering the hardships. Then he brightened. 'But a man with a bit put by, now, can buy himself a piece of land and settle down. Maybe even get a decent woman to marry him and share it.'

Kate nodded briskly, approving of his ambition, but Ginger hooted with laughter.

'Knew you was going soft, Kilkenny. You sound as if you was almost in your grave. Give me rampaging any day! And women that *aren't* decent. Who wants to settle down?'

Jem echoed that in his mind. There was a flicker of disappointment with Conor there, a feeling as though he had been let down by the navvy's humdrum dream.

Conor felt the silence he had brought on by this solemn confession and, whipping the pipe to his lips, he swept the quietness away with the romping twists of an

Irish jig, setting their feet beating time. When the tune came to an end, he rounded quickly on Kate.

'It's mean you are with your hospitality, Miss Penfold.'

'Oh?' She was suddenly sharp and awkward again, not knowing what to expect.

'With a voice the like of yours, you should be singing to us.'

There was no mistaking his firmness. Jem chuckled to himself to hear Kate being bullied. A taste of her own medicine. But at the same time he waited for her to open her mouth and shrivel Conor with a chilly word.

But she did not. She gave a queer little smile, flushed beetroot colour and said, 'What would you fancy hearing?'

'What ever you like. I can pick the tune up and follow on my whistle.'

Quickly, as though fearing to lose her courage, she plunged straight into one of the village songs.

> 'Mother, mother make my bed,
> And wrap me in a milk-white sheet . . .'

The notes of the whistle copied plainly at first and then, with runs and long-drawn trills, decorated the tune that Jem knew so well. Kate sat stiff upright, the baby on her lap, not looking at any of them. But the song caught hold of her as it did of her listeners, and her voice slowed plaintively in the last verse.

> 'This rose and the briar, they grew up together,
> Till they could grow no higher.
> They met at the top in a true lovers' knot
> And the rose it clung round the sweet briar.'

Just for a second they held it amongst them in silence, the feeling she had given them. Then she shattered it

herself, standing up and saying briskly, 'Fine enough
goings on for lords and ladies, maybe, but queer ones for
folks that have just stuck a pig.'

Jem felt it like a smack on the face. That was always
the way with Kate. If she felt you soften, she would
slam you with her hardness, so that you should know
that she was stronger than you were. He was bitter with
himself for being tricked into it after all these years.

But Conor was not abashed. He looked steadily at her,
a laugh in his eye.

'And haven't folks that stick pigs a right to fine
feelings of their own?'

Not used to being challenged, she just shrugged
sulkily and made for the stairs. But Conor did not mean
to let her escape. He held out his whistle towards her.
'It's a pity that someone with an ear the like of yours for
a good tune hasn't the skill of this whistle. Come over
here and try your hand at it now.' She made an
impatient movement. 'No, let the lad take the baby.'

Ginger raised himself from where he sat half-asleep.
'That's it. She should have a go. This young shaver'll
take the little 'un.' And he gave Jem a shove in the back,
so that the boy found himself across the room and half-
way up the stairs with Martha before he knew what he
was doing. When he had settled her in her cradle, he
came downstairs to find Kate still playing hoity toity,
although less stiffly now, and he dared a joke at her.

'Beg your *pardon*. No one told me a grand lady had
come calling. Evening, Mrs Neville.'

At the mention of the Rector's wife, Kate tossed her
head and reached out for the whistle. Conor watched,
with a grin. She brought shrill squeals out of the pipe,
while her fingers scuttled helplessly over the holes, and
Ginger covered his ears in pretended pain.

'I can't,' she said at last. 'You see?'

'And isn't it the simplest thing in the whole world?' Conor's tone was a mixture of amusement and exasperation. 'Forget these two rude fellows,' he jerked his head at Jem and Ginger, who were chuckling at each other, 'and keep your mind on your fingers. Will I show you?'

He went to stand behind her, his arms one on either side to guide her fingers. Instantly she was bright red again and for a moment the notes came in a chaotic cluster, but Con meant to teach her. He led her through the notes and up and down the scale until, at last, she played half a tune.

Lowering the pipe, she turned triumphantly to face him as he beamed down at her. 'Didn't I tell you then?' he said, and the two of them began to laugh as if it were the funniest thing in the world. Ginger, dozing by the fire, woke up and, catching the mood if not its cause, joined in. Watching the three of them, Jem suddenly wished that the villagers could see. Perhaps the sight of happiness, with no riot or rampaging, would do away with the hatred so that there need be no fight on Sunday. With that thought he shivered, remembering that he was promised to cheer for Joe, whatever his own wishes might be. There would be no joy for him in this fight and in the middle of the others' laughter he stood solemn, thinking of Sunday and dreading it.

Uncannily, as if echoing his thoughts, Kate gulped down her laughter and said, 'Sunday.'

'Sunday?' Conor and Ginger calmed down and looked polite and enquiring.

'The pig feast.' She said it as if it were obvious, as though Sunday could mean nothing else. 'We've no kin to ask. And I'd not have the village folk even if they wanted. But will the two of you come? You've helped us a lot today.'

She was serious now, the hostess, and Conor copied her mood. Gravely he answered for the two of them. 'We'll be honoured, Miss Penfold. A grand idea.' It was the formal politeness of the message he had sent her from the cutting, and it sounded odd in the middle of their friendliness and laughter, but Kate smiled and her eyes followed him as he went to the gate with Ginger to say goodnight. It was almost a minute before she turned to order Jem to bed.

Jem slept badly that night, and his dreams were plagued with fear. He saw Kate and Conor mixing a huge black pudding, their arms red to the elbow, giggling and teasing each other as they stirred. Through the door, the smith watched frowning, his hammer poised to batter them, but Jem could do nothing to stop him because he was carrying a huge mound of pigmeat to distribute to the neighbours. And when he opened his mouth to shout a warning, something quite different came out. All he could say in his dream was, 'How could Kate be such a . . . such a *girl*?'

He woke with a sense of danger, but nothing in real life seemed to answer to his dream except the thing he could have prophesied anyway, the distribution of the pigmeat. And even that was no mound. Kate, her gentle mood vanished with the darkness, sniffed and said that she would send no meat to those who had refused their help. Which left very few. Only the two old widows up the end of the village, and the family at the Rectory. Kate picked out the joints as soon as Conor was off up to the line and pushed Jem out to deliver them while she got on with putting the most part of the pig in pickle.

Jem went first to the two old women. That was simple. They were poor enough to make no fuss, brightening when they saw the meat and sending kind messages back to Kate. But, that done, there was Mary

Ann to see at the Rectory, and the thought of her bossiness and her mistress's views on navvies brought back all the bruises of Jem's dealings with the village on Saturday. His knock at the door of the Rectory kitchen was hesitant.

Mary Ann opened it with a smile, but when she saw who had knocked her face fell into solemn creases.

'Jem Penfold. What do you want here?'

'We killed the pig last afternoon.' He thrust at her the neat, muslin-covered bundle that Kate had made up. Mary Ann looked at it dubiously.

'Well, it's a kind thought, and I'm sure Mrs Neville will be pleased to see such gratitude. Very proper of your sister. But I'm not sure I'd do right to take it. The Rector, now. He's very put out about this navvy you've got staying. Very put out.'

Jem listened to her prosing on about the Rector for a moment. But he could see that she was set to take the meat. She was just using the chance to lecture him, and suddenly he bristled at it. ' . . . the Rector's very particular about these things. I'm not sure he'll—'

'Aw, take it!' Jem pushed the damp bundle into her arms and made off down the path. When he got to the gate he turned and grinned into her stupid, startled face. 'Tell Rector it'll do his stomach a power of good!'

CHAPTER SEVEN

Sitting in church next Sunday morning, his mind full of the afternoon's fight, Jem looked around almost disbelievingly. The villagers were showing their usual blank, scrubbed faces to the gentry. Seeing those solemn expressions, no one who did not know could have guessed at the fierceness of the scene in the forge when the fight was being planned. The men, stiff in their Sunday suits, seemed like stuffed things with no feelings of their own. Hoppy Noyce stooped in a back pew and Elijah Day nodded in a front one, his sharp little mother nudging him in the ribs. Towering over them all was Joe Hamage, washed from the grime of the forge and newly shaved. He looked like a huge baby, bland and pink, and his eyes opened wide at the sermon, as if every word spoke to his heart.

Not that it could have done. Up in the pulpit Mr Neville was preaching his usual sort of sermon, fluttering papers, flapping his hands and ruffling his hair. He was a good man. The villagers were fond of him. But even on a normal Sunday no one could have listened to his sermons. That day, perhaps sensing an odd feeling in the air, he struggled harder, flung up his hands more earnestly, sent white showers of paper down from the pulpit on to the people in the front rows. But no one understood. No one listened. What had old parson's hand-flappings and his bits of Greek to do with their potatoes, their rents, and the fight that afternoon?

Underneath the ordinary Sunday calmness, Jem could feel a tension, as though everyone in the village were waiting for the end of the day. But no one said anything. No one looked at him. He and Kate sat half-way down the church in an island not connected to the rest of the village.

The Rector's wife and daughter left the church before everyone else, Mrs Neville sweeping past Kate with her eyes deliberately turned away. She had made a point of ignoring the Penfolds ever since Kate had spoken her mind. Miss Ellen stopped for a short moment beside their pew, ready to speak to them, but an impatient backward look from her mother drew her away with no more than a shrug.

After them the villagers made their way out, more silently than usual, muttering and separating hurriedly. Only Kate and Jem came out alone.

Getting back to the cottage was like bursting up through the surface of water into fresh air and sunlight. Conor and Ginger, left to mind the baby, were stretched out in chairs on either side of the fire. Conor never went to church with the Penfolds although he was often in the house of a Sunday morning. He claimed to be a Catholic, but they had never known him go to Mass. Ginger, who had arrived just as Kate and Jem were leaving, had been invited to go with them, but he had only chuckled.

'Haven't been since I was christened, Miss Penfold. Proper damp it was too. Couldn't risk another visit.'

Kate had gone off with a sniff of disapproval, but now, coming in out of the silence, she smiled as broad as Jem at their silly chatter.

Smiled and at once caught up her apron, tying it tightly round her waist.

'Jem. Get down to the bakehouse for the pies. Mr O'Flynn, would you give me a hand with this pot?' It was a volley of crisp orders. Only to Ginger she would not speak, because she did not like to call him Ginger and she did not know any other name for him.

When Jem staggered in with the two big pies, which had been pulled out of the bakehouse oven by a silent and embarrassed Elijah, he found the two navvies already at the table, leaning back and smiling. Conor sniffed.

'Ah. I've not smelt the like of that these many years.'

Kate glanced up from her serving, almost pert. 'Likely. They say you all live on sides of best beef up at the camp.'

'Terrible it is, the good food that's wasted up there. Good food in plenty, but no one to do more than throw it in the pot and wish. Never a cook the likes of you.'

Pink with pleasure, Kate handed them platefuls of food and they started to eat, not wasting any breath by talking. For a while, Jem could think of nothing but the rich taste of the fresh pigmeat, but gradually he noticed something else. Unobtrusively, in spite of his fine words, Conor was eating as little as he could. Catching Jem's eye on him, he smiled rather sheepishly. 'It wouldn't do to be going to the fight with my belly bulging, would it now?'

Kate put her knife down slowly. But it was Jem who spoke.

'Who is it, Con?' he said quickly. 'Who's fighting Joe?'

It was Ginger who answered, unaware of the expression on Kate's face. 'Kilkenny here, of course. Who'd you think?'

'Fight?' It was the old, stiff Kate, her voice tight with anger. 'What fight?'

Con watched her carefully. 'The lad's not told you?'

'No one told me.'

He shrugged uneasily. 'Sure, it's only a bit of fun now. A match between one of us and one of them.'

'Fun? FUN?' She rose to her feet and stormed down at them. 'Haven't you seen the village folk this last month? Are they thinking of *fun*?'

'It'll be fine,' Conor said soothingly, but she walked away towards the scullery. At the door she said, without turning, 'He'll kill you.'

She slammed the door. They could hear her moving about outside and the food on the table, so splendid a moment ago, took on a sour smell, a greasy look. Con pulled out a pipe and lit it. Only when it was drawing properly did he turn to Jem.

'Tell us about this fellow, then.'

Jem had been measuring Con against the blacksmith in his mind, unhappily, and now he said cautiously, 'You've seen him.'

'I've seen he's a big man. Can he fight, now?'

'He's got a big fist.' Jem wriggled uneasily. 'He's the champion. And he means no good to you.'

Conor blew a smoke ring and stared at it. 'I never fought a man that did. How should I deal with him, then? Me being so weak and all?'

Jem smiled feebly at the joke. 'Well . . . he's big, but he's heavy. Lumpish on his feet.' He stopped, unable to think of anything else. Ginger pulled his chair closer in impatience.

'Come on then. Don't go drying up.' He obviously liked fighting talk better than scenes. 'Spill the beans. What's the bloke's soft spot?'

But Conor had a shrewd eye on Jem. 'Never mind now, lad. That'll do to start with,' he said quietly.

'Kilkenny!' Ginger protested. 'Come off it. Sounds like you could do with all the help that's going.'

'Shut your mouth now, Ginger. The lad's a village

lad. Maybe he's not for us at all. Had you thought of that now?'

Jem ran a finger round inside his scarf, his neck hot with guilt, and stammered, 'There's no choice. He made me say I'd shout for him.' He wanted to explain, but it would have been weak, like excusing himself.

Conor only laughed. 'Is it the end of the world then? Will I break my heart if you shout for someone else?' Then he added, more seriously, 'It's hard for you, I'm thinking, between us from the line and them in the village.'

Jem was embarrassed. Half of him felt comforted that Conor had noticed, but the other half felt strange, as if the Irishman had been spying on him. 'Hadn't you best go?' he asked gruffly.

Ginger leapt to his feet in relief and clapped Conor on the back. 'On your feet, Kilkenny. Let's get up there and show these villagers what real men are like!'

Conor stood up quietly and gestured with his hand at the scullery door. 'Your sister. Will she be wanting to come?'

Jem knocked and called. 'Kate. We're going.'

She bounced out, still three-quarters in a rage. 'Be off with you then. Get this foolishness over.'

'You coming?'

She sniffed. 'That'll be no place for a respectable woman. I'll stay where I am.' She hesitated for a moment, and then went on, 'But you get up there, lad. Might as well see fair play for Mr O'Flynn.' It was said grudgingly, as if it were all she could squeeze out of herself, but Conor thanked her for it, and for the pig feast, as graciously as he would if she had made him a pretty speech.

The two men and the boy set off together up the slope towards the Copse, walking in silence. Half-way up, Con stopped and motioned Jem to go ahead by himself. The boy turned awkwardly.

'Good luck.'

Conor smiled and held out his hand. 'Away you go, then. I'll be up in a minute to get a sight of this terrible man.'

Jem plunged upwards into the Copse and came out on the other side into a crowd. Or, rather, two crowds, for the split was clear. The village men huddled together close by the trees talking softly. In the middle of the group was the massive figure of Joe, the smith, stripped to the waist, huge and square, listening with half his attention to the advice and encouragement that came at him from all sides. The navvies stood higher up the hill. Not all of them were there—not even all those from the nearest camp—but there must have been at least sixty or seventy. Round the edge of the group fluttered a few slatternly women, draggled but brightly dressed in garish finery. The navvies were talking loudly as they watched for Conor, joshing each other and shouting aloud with laughter. From the middle of the group rose the unmistakable foreign voice of Pigtail.

Jem hovered on the edge of the village group, not liking to leave it, but not able to join it properly because the men ignored him, with their backs turned.

As Con came up through the trees, the navvies gave a welcoming shout and crowded forwards, cheering him and slapping him on the back as if he had already won. And Joe Hamage acknowledged his presence with a sneering shout: 'I thought they were sending us a *proper* man.' But Conor himself stayed quiet, looking the blacksmith up and down with a thoughtful eye.

Within five minutes the men had all formed a rough circle, thin where the two groups touched each other, but crowded and jostling everywhere else. Jem placing himself in one of the spaces, between navvies and villagers, listened to the talk around him.

'Who've they got to referee, then?'

'That's the fellow from the inn over Little Morden way. Reckon he'll want to keep in with both sides if he can.'

'Fair enough. They doing best of three falls?'

'No. In rounds, they're fighting. Till one gets knocked out or cries quits.'

Jem whistled softly when he heard this piece of information. A hard fight, then. And the mood of the crowd was hardening to match it. There was none of the cheerful joking he remembered from the matches his father had fought in the village. Here, there was a gathering silence, tense and watchful.

Then the two big men were alone in the ring, circling each other. Joe stood half a head taller than Conor and was broad to match. The Irishman moved confidently and carefully, but Jem's heart sank and he clenched his fists deep in his pockets.

'Come on, Kilkenny! Show him a few!' The first shout sparked them off, and both sides erupted into roars of encouragement as the men closed with each other. At first it seemed as if the smith would overwhelm the navvy at once, by sheer weight, but Con stayed light on his feet, twisting out of every clench, evading the bigger man without, yet, attacking him. At the end of the first round, a few jeers came from the villagers, but Conor returned to his corner undisturbed and talked quietly to Ginger.

Joe, in the opposite corner, flexed his arms dramatically and then strode over to Jem. The boy tried to cower back into the crowd, but there were not enough people where he stood, and the village men pushed him forward.

Joe grinned down at him, confident and ugly. 'I've not heard any cheers from you.'

'I . . . I—' Jem wished with all his heart that he could speak out and say he would do what he liked, but the smith was too near and too big. His courage shrivelled.

'Louder, boy, louder,' said Joe with relish. 'You wouldn't want me out of temper with you, would you?'

Jem nodded weakly and gazed at his boots, pink-faced, until the next round began.

The next two or three rounds showed clearly what was in Conor's mind. He was set to tire the smith by keeping him always on the move, by feinting and wriggling out of holds. Once or twice he misjudged and was engulfed by the smith's enormous arms. Once it was even worse. Joe had him on the ground and was sitting on his chest, banging his head with obvious pleasure. Jem dug his nails into the palms of his hands and shouted as loudly as he could. All he could shout— all he dared shout—was 'Joe! Come on!' but he shouted it furiously, hoping that Conor would understand that it was meant for him. In fact, it was not possible that Conor could have heard him. His boy's voice was lost in the roars of the navvies and the triumphant yells of the villagers. For a moment it seemed as though the fight must be all over but, with a shove that knotted all his muscles, Conor tumbled the smith and scrambled up to survive the rest of the round.

As the noise died at the end of the round, lowering to murmurs, Jem heard something unexpected behind, familiar but out of place. A baby's cry. He glanced over his shoulder at the Copse. At first he could see nothing, but then a slight movement caught his eye. Almost hidden among the trees was a figure in a checked shawl. A shawl that he knew well.

He nearly ran to the Copse to pull her forwards, so much did he long for company. With Kate at his elbow he would have felt braver, not so isolated. But just as he began to move he caught another glimpse of her lurking figure and something held him back. It seemed unkind to tear her out of her hiding place. With an effort, he shut his mouth and turned back to watch the fight.

It was a long fight. The smith was slow to tire, and a lot of Conor's time was spent simply evading him. But gradually his lurches became wilder and less controlled. The first time Conor threw him, the villagers fell silent. Even Jem was a little awed. He had once seen his father put Joe on the ground, by luck more than anything else, but no one else had thrown him these ten years and the villagers had come to think of it as an impossibility. It was like seeing an oak tree tumbled.

Joe leapt back on to his feet with a bellow of rage and launched himself wildly at Conor. But almost before he could draw breath he was on his back again. After that, the outcome was inevitable. The smith lost his temper, and any lingering shreds of judgement went with it. Conor, still cool and controlled, dominated the fight now. The next time Joe stampeded forward he was thrown again and this time he landed badly, his head flung back.

'Come on, Joe!' Ten or twelve desperate voices were still sounding for him, but not all the villagers' shouts could drag him to his feet by the end of the count. He lay flat on his back with glazed eyes, almost unconscious.

Then the navvies opened their throats in a great howl of delight, and two of their women pushed into the ring, even before the count was finished, throwing themselves on Conor with hugs and kisses, their shawls falling back off their dishevelled hair. As soon as the count was over, the ring melted into a pushing, shoving mass of people and Jem was thrown backwards and forwards, buffeted by the elbows of everyone who wanted to clap the winner on the back. Conor grinned cheerfully at them, his chest pumping as he gasped for breath and scrubbed his hot face with a neckerchief. Then he jostled his way through to the smith, who had just heaved on to hands and knees.

'Will you shake hands now? I'm proud to have fought a man the like of you.'

Joe rose ominously to his feet. It was twilight now, and he stood in the half-darkness like a monolithic stone, his eyes travelling over the Irishman with an expression of contempt. At last, with the slowness of insult, he said, 'A coward's fight that was. And a filthy Irish trick that won it.' Gathering his mouth together, he spat full into Conor's face.

An angry roar went up from the navvies, but they were held in check by Conor's utter stillness as he watched the smith leave the hillside. Joe pushed roughly through the crowd and stormed past Jem, near enough to touch but without a glance.

Only when Jem saw Ben following behind with his father's shirt did he realize that his friend had been there all the time. He opened his mouth to say something sympathetic; he had no quarrel with Ben. But his friend walked past with his face turned so rigidly away that he must have known who was watching him. It was like a blow in the face, and Jem could feel himself flinching.

Only when the smith and his son had disappeared into the Copse did Conor lift the neckerchief and slowly wipe the spit from his cheek. At once, the babble broke out again.

'And why didn't you put one on him, Kilkenny?'

'Let's be after him!'

'Come on, lads!'

Conor shook his head authoritatively. 'There was no shame to losing a fight the like of that. If a man takes it badly, it's shame to him and none to me. You all saw I beat him fair and square.'

Even the villagers seemed to agree with that, for instead of muttering rebelliously they melted away one by one, embarrassed by their champion. Jem glanced back at the Copse, but there was no sign of Kate's checked shawl. He found himself hoping that she had left as soon as the fight was over and had missed seeing Conor stand to be insulted without fighting back. With half his mind, Jem could see the sense of it, but with the other half he wanted to see Conor hammer Joe into the ground and beat the swaggering look from his face. It would have been some return, even though a sour one, for his own pain in the forge on the night the fight was planned.

But now the smith was gone and the winner was buttoning his shirt and tying his neckerchief. Catching Jem's eye he beckoned him over with a grin.

'There you are, lad. I heard you cheering. Fine and loud it was.'

Jem knew that he was being teased, but he could see the eyes of the other navvies on him, some curious and a few hostile. Pigtail's black eyes were glittering maliciously. Jem looked down awkwardly and kicked at a clod of earth. 'I wouldn't—'

'Sure and there's no harm done.'

Ginger's hand came heavy on the boy's shoulder. 'You coming up the camp? We're off to celebrate.'

At once Jem's awkwardness vanished in a surge of pride. It had always been his dream to be asked up to the camp like a grown man, and he could feel a silly grin spreading over his face as he opened his mouth to reply.

But before he could say anything Conor broke in. 'Your sister—'

It was true and Jem knew it. Kate would be beside herself if she knew he was going to the camp. But all the same, it irked him to be reminded of it, like a child.

As though to give him an excuse to refuse, Conor said gently, 'Won't she be wanting to know how the fight went?'

For a moment Jem was tempted to say that she knew already, that she had seen it all. He knew that if he did the men would take him up to the camp with them. But the same thing that had held him back before did so again and, hardly knowing why he did so, he took the let-out that Conor had given him.

'I'll be off home to tell her, then.'

'Good lad.' The Irishman beamed his approval as the men turned away up the hill in a great dark crowd, the bright shawls of the women fluttering round the edges. Hovering by the Copse to watch them go, Jem saw them for a moment as part of a huge army, always on the move, only passing through. Only, instead of burning and death, they left behind them shining rails and steaming engines. Still thinking, he turned back to the village.

Kate was sitting in the rocking-chair as always on a Sunday, with the house tidy and her hands tight-clasped in her lap. Jem had sometimes fancied that it was only by holding one in the other that she could prevent them from wriggling away of their own accord to scrub floors or wash windows. The baby was sleeping peacefully in the cradle, silent except for an occasional grunt. The two of them looked, thought Jem admiringly, as though they had not stirred these three hours.

'A good fight?' Kate was able to sound languidly uninterested.

'Not bad.' He sat down to take off his boots. If she wanted to pretend she didn't care, let her pretend. She knew anyway.

After a bit she said, 'Joe win?'

'No.'

'Oh. Mr O'Flynn did well?'

'Yes.' Jem flicked up his eyes and caught her watching him. 'Good view from the Copse?'

For a moment they stared at each other defiantly, both knowing. Then Kate said carelessly, 'Like as not. Anyone there?'

Jem smiled slowly and shook his head. As he did so, it came to him that he had joined her in a secret. She knew that he had not told and that he would not tell. It was the first time for years that there had been anything more between them than the shared need to eat and keep a roof over them, and he was amazed at the sudden warm feeling it gave him.

CHAPTER EIGHT

In the days that followed, Jem learnt to count the full cost of the fight he had sparked off, as he stood crow-keeping in the cold fields, shaking the heavy wooden clapper. His 'Holla Ca-whoo! Ca-whoo!' sounded emptily over the mud and no friendly face peered through the gate to call a greeting or ask after the baby. Only the birds, flying black off the seed-corn when he chased, cawed mockingly in his face. From the moment he left the cottage before dawn to the moment he returned after dusk, the only voice he heard was the farmer's, giving him orders. Those villagers who had to pass him turned their faces away or grunted a half-greeting without meeting his eyes. All his shouting for Joe had been wasted effort, for the plain verdict of the village was that the Penfolds had taken the navvies' side.

Kate made no comment on the silence. She had never been one to waste time gossiping or drinking tea with the other women in the village, and spending her days alone was not strange to her. Only, her lips folded tighter together and her temper was sourer than usual. And Jem noticed that whenever she needed advice about the baby she walked to the Rectory to brave Mary Ann's wordy disapproval rather than call on one of their neighbours. But neither Kate nor Jem said anything to Conor and, coming back late of an evening, he did not guess.

As Christmas grew nearer, the loneliness seemed to lie heavier on them, for they could look forward to no festival. In her prickliness, Kate had even squashed Conor's hesitant suggestion that they should all spend the day together. She had told him that she would expect him to take himself off to the grand feast that the navvies were planning, up on the Beacon, and she had refused his invitation to join in. Jem could see that there was nothing in store for them but a bleak and silent Christmas.

A week before Christmas, he and Kate were startled by a sound that had become unfamiliar to them. A knock at the cottage door. They glanced at each other questioningly before she went to open it.

When she did they were even more surprised, for there outside, twisting her reticule in nervous hands, stood the Rector's daughter.

'Hallo, Kate,' she said, and then stood irresolutely on the threshold.

'Come in out of the cold, then,' said Kate, a trifle impatiently, and Miss Ellen stepped inside and stood speechless.

'Over here by the fire.' Kate shut the door and propelled her visitor briskly to a stool. Then she stood still, waiting. At last Miss Ellen spoke, in a jerky voice.

'Perhaps you think it strange that I should come here alone. Because I never have.'

'It's kind of you to spare time,' Kate said, prim and wary, sitting down on the stool opposite. Miss Ellen gave her reticule another twist.

'I thought . . . that is . . . I don't wish to meddle, but I couldn't help noticing how things are for your family.'

'Yes?' Kate looked at her crushingly, but she plunged on with the force of a shy person who has finally summoned the courage to speak.

'I see how no one talks to you any more coming out of church, and I hear the things they say about you to Mamma when we visit them.'

Kate looked frigidly at her. 'I pay no heed to gossip.'

'Oh, I know! I know!' Miss Ellen floundered for a moment and then leaned forward earnestly. 'Please don't take this amiss. I've always been fond of your family. When I was a child I hated going visiting with Mamma, but your mother was kind to me. She talked to me and gave me cups of milk.'

'She was a good woman,' nodded Kate, a little softened by this praise of her mother.

'Well—I wanted to do something for you. If I can.'

'We can get by without charity, miss.'

It was an unkind thing to say and Kate must have realized it when Miss Ellen went pink, for she added more gently, 'But thank you kindly for asking.'

'The line, Kate,' Miss Ellen burst out awkwardly, 'it won't go on for ever, you know. They say it will be finished in a few months. What will you do then?'

Again Jem saw in his mind the picture of the dark army of navvies marching away into the distance, but this time it came home to him that Conor would be one of them, that he would move on when the line was finished. Hastily he pushed the thought to the back of his mind.

Kate seemed to do the same, for she said briskly, 'We'll deal with that in God's good time.'

Miss Ellen got up abruptly and stood facing her without speaking. Jem looked at them. Two girls. Of an age, but different in every other way. One delicate and upright, dressed in clothes whose price would have fed the Penfolds for months, and the other bony and reddened, too thin for her darned and inherited dress. Miss Ellen put out her narrow, white hand and timidly touched Kate's rough one.

'When that happens,' she said with deliberation, 'when they do go, I will stand your friend. Do not forget. Goodbye.'

Suddenly Kate moved her fingers to grip the other girl's hand. 'I'll not forget. Thank you, miss. Goodbye.'

Her face had softened, but she said no more and, as soon as Miss Ellen had gone, she turned to snap at Jem as if nothing had happened.

But it was obvious that Miss Ellen's words had made some kind of impression, for a change came over Kate's conversations with Conor. She had come to be friendly, and even merry, when speaking to him, and she continued so in general, but whenever he spoke of the railways she answered sourly, as if not wishing to be reminded of what had brought him. He endured her sourness without comment until a few days before Christmas, when he came home full of excitement because work had finally started on the long tunnel under one side of the Beacon. The tunnel was at once the hardest and the most spectacular piece of work on the line, and Conor began to describe it enthusiastically.

'Lot of grown men grubbing round in the earth,' Kate muttered.

He looked at her quietly and said at last, 'It's plain you've taken against the railway. And why would that be?'

She went on sewing, not looking up. 'Load of stupid nonsense. Why would a person want to be rushed about that way? We're well enough where we are.'

Suddenly Conor's eyes flashed, and Jem remembered how passionately he had talked of the railway on the day they had first met. Now he fired up in the same way, bursting out at Kate as he never had before. 'And you with never an idea of what a railway is like! You've never seen an engine in full steam, I'll be bound.'

She shrugged. 'You don't pine for what you've never had.'

'But you *shall* have it.' There was an unusual authority in his voice. 'I told you, didn't I, that they've opened the branch to Lingport already? Well, you'll come with me after Christmas to ride on it. And the boy. I'll take you both, and afterwards you can sneer at it if you've a fancy to. What do you say?'

Jem sat bolt upright, willing her to say 'Yes', but she tossed her head.

'How can I? There's the child.'

'Faith and we'll take her too.' The prospect of the outing had restored Conor's customary good temper and Kate was no match for him. Every objection she found he cheerfully demolished, and it was agreed at last that they should make the trip after Christmas when the weather grew brighter.

It was good to have something to look forward to over that Christmas. Thanks to Kate's pride, it passed like one of the bleak days before Conor's coming, with the brother and sister watching each other over their meals, unable to think of anything to say.

But Christmas mattered nothing to Jem in comparison with the promised journey on the railway. He missed Ben badly in the few weeks before they went. It would have doubled his pleasure if they could have talked it over and speculated about what it would be like. And how Ben would have envied him, in spite of everything! But all his longing for a companion could not drive him to the forge to seek Ben out. He could imagine only too well the kind of reception that would greet him. Nevertheless, even without the spur of Ben's envy, Jem became furiously excited. On the night before they went, he tossed and turned so much in bed that even Conor, who was placid and slept heavily, growled at him to lie still.

They rose at five the next morning. At six they had to

set off to walk the eight miles to Helmston, where they would catch the train. After gulping down a piece of bread, Jem went out to the well to wash. Kate came and stood over him.

'Aw, give over, Kate. I'm old enough.'

'*And* back of your ears.'

He splashed about in the cold until she pulled him impatiently from the well.

'Set your hair straight, now. And there's your good smock on the dresser.'

He went in and pulled it over his damp hair to cover the odd collection of shirts and waistcoats that he had amassed to keep him warm in the fields. It was sharply cold outside, in spite of the sun, and even in the cottage his breath steamed whitely. Kate bustled in.

'There's your cap. And you'd best take Dad's old scarf.'

'Aw, Kate. Don't bundle me.'

'Go on. You'll freeze solid else, sitting still in the train.'

She was bundled herself, in a thick old coat of her mother's, a muffler, and matted woollen mittens. The baby, in shawls and shawls, was like a parcel. Jem began to giggle.

'Fine family we are. Like a load of old washing.'

'Never you mind, Jem Penfold. Better that than catch your death.'

But she looked down doubtfully at herself and almost sighed as she pulled on her battered old bonnet over the hair she had—for once—brushed to a gleam and coiled smoothly. As though to herself, she said firmly, 'Poor folks are poor folks. Doesn't do no good to go pretending.'

'And aren't you all a lovely sight?'

It was Conor, emerging from the door at the bottom of the stairs. A vision to make them blink. His hair was

slicked down shinily and in one hand, ready to set
rakishly upon his head, was a new white felt hat. His
other hand he kept behind his back. Never was there
such a fine, velvety square-tailed jacket as the one which
draped his broad shoulders. Never was there such a
bright waistcoat as the one which spread across his
chest. His moleskin breeches were brushed into
smartness and his boots polished like mirrors. Some of
the clothes were, perhaps, a thought crumpled from
being stored so long in his bag, but the expression on
the Penfolds' faces must have shown him that they did
not notice. He flung back his head and laughed.

'Have you never seen a navvy-man dressed in his
best? Isn't it a splendid thing, to be sure?'

'Too grand for us, maybe,' said Kate. She made it
sound like a joke, but his face went suddenly grave.

'Indeed, that's foolish. Like I said, you're all of you
looking grand. But . . .' and here he looked a little
sheepish, 'seeing it's a holiday I've taken the liberty of
getting you a small present.'

From behind his back he fetched out a bonnet. And
such a bonnet. It was bright purple plush, adorned with
bunches of violets and plumes of emerald green and
furnished with wide green ribbons to tie under the chin.
Kate stared. Jem stared. Neither of them had ever seen a
bonnet anything like it.

'Don't you like it, then?' Conor sounded almost hurt
and Kate, who had just opened her mouth to protest
that she could not possibly accept such a present, said
briskly, 'It's a fine bonnet. Much too fine for the likes of
me, maybe.'

'Nothing's too fine for you, Miss Penfold.' The words
were cheerful, but there was a certain anxiety behind
them, a fear that the present might be rejected. Kate
heard it and at once reached out her hand for the bonnet.

'Thank you very much.'

She took it from him and he disappeared upstairs again, muttering that he had forgotten something. Jem looked at Kate.

'You're never going to wear it?'

'What? Of course I am.' And she went across to the broken scrap of mirror on the dresser, took off her old black bonnet and set the amazing new one on her neat brown hair.

'But, Kate, it's—' Jem wriggled awkwardly, not knowing quite why it embarrassed him to see her prim face under those extravagant feathers. Then it came to him. 'You look like a tally-woman.' That was what they were called, the women who hung round the navvies and lived in the camp. He had heard the village men talk of them. How could Kate—? But she sniffed.

'No one's going to take *me* for a tally-woman.'

She twitched and fiddled at the bonnet as though nothing in the world could have pleased her more. Coming once more through the door at the bottom of the stairs, Conor looked at her with great satisfaction.

'The colour suits you fine.'

'Thank you, Mr O'Flynn,' she said, her voice colourless but her cheeks pink.

Then they were off. Jem carried the bundle with their bread and cheese for lunch, and Conor and Kate took it in turns to take the baby, who was beginning to weigh heavy now, a fine, healthy, six-months' child.

It took them nearly three hours to walk to Helmston, and every step of the way was a delight to Jem, for Kate was in good spirits, stepping out like the country girl she was with her cheeks pink under the green and purple, and Conor was full of songs and stories, teasing Kate and feeding Jem's appetite for marvels. As they came close to their destination, the Irishman drew in a great breath of air.

'The sea! Can't you smell it?'

Kate and Jem sniffed hard, Kate holding the baby up as if she too could join in, and indeed there was a certain something about the air, a strangeness.

'Where is it?' Jem began to feel excited. 'Where's the sea?'

Conor looked amused. 'Have you never seen it, then?'

Jem shook his head. 'Only from far off. From up top of the Beacon.'

'Nor have I,' added Kate, her eyes sparkling now.

Conor was amazed. 'And you only eight miles away. Isn't there an ounce of adventure in you?'

Kate looked faintly surprised. 'Why should we come to Helmston? We've nothing to sell here.'

'To see it all!' Conor almost shouted at her, flinging his arms wide to take in the town, the sea ahead of them and the sky above. 'Why, I've walked the length and breadth of England these last ten years, since I first landed in Liverpool.'

Jem gaped at him. 'On your own feet?'

'Not on my hands, lad, to be sure. A fine fool I'd have looked.' And, touched by the spirit of holiday, he flipped suddenly from his feet to his hands and strutted into Helmston upside-down.

Jem gulped with laughter, and Kate's lips twitched in spite of herself, but she hurried after, saying in a low voice, 'Mr O'Flynn! People are staring!'

And so they were, if 'people' meant a few raggy children who cheered and ran along beside. At her reprimand Conor at once came right side up—much to Jem's regret—and apologized soberly. 'I'd no mind to make a spectacle of you.'

Kate, in her turn, seemed put out with herself for objecting. 'I—'

'Oh, come *on!*' Jem interrupted impatiently. 'The sea! Let's go to the sea!'

When he stood in front of it, it almost stopped his breath. It was more different than he could have imagined from the neat patch of blue or grey he had always seen from the Beacon. Close to, it was vast and alive, constantly moving and glittering, and it gave him the same feeling of freedom as the Beacon did, a feeling of wanting to run until his legs failed and to gulp down lungfuls of air. His limbs tingled and he almost shouted, 'I can do anything!'

Conor left them undisturbed for a few minutes and then he said, 'Come on, for the train won't wait.'

If a feeling had crossed Jem's mind that the railway might be a disappointment after the sea, that was quickly dispelled. Conor led the Penfolds briskly through crowds that bewildered them, past houses that awed them, until they came into the station.

'There you are, then!' He flung his arms wide and they looked.

A grand front gave into the hall of the station, which stretched upwards immensely high, in delicate pillars of iron arching up and up. Jem had never imagined a building so large and, at the same time, so airy and he stood with his head flung back, goggling. There was a hissing of steam and a babble of talk. Most of the station was empty, in fact, for only the branch line was finished and opened, but to Jem's village eyes and ears the whole thing seemed crowded and confusing.

When Conor took them to see the engine, Jem found once again that the reality outstripped his imagination. The puff of steam and the gleam of metal he had thought of, but not the huge size, nor the noise. He smiled at his own silliness, and Conor looked at him questioningly.

'Good enough for you?'

'I thought,' Jem looked at his boots, 'I thought it would be something the size of a cart-horse.'

Conor roared with laughter. 'Would we be making all this fuss about something the size of a cart-horse? No, lad, it's a powerful thing.'

'I looked for it to be dirty,' Kate said thoughtfully. 'All that steam and smoke.'

'And so it would,' said Conor, 'only the driver keeps it polished up. Fair proud of their engines they are.'

The locomotive let out a shuddering hiss of steam and Kate jumped backwards.

'Is it safe?'

'As safe as a stroll up the lane,' Conor said soothingly, 'and ten times as safe as a horse and cart. Would I take you, now, if it was dangerous?'

He shepherded them down the train towards the third-class coaches. To begin with, Jem found these a little disappointing. The first- and second-class carriages were much grander, with roofs on top and windows and doors. Third-class passengers had to make do with open trucks and wooden benches. Once he was inside, however, curiosity swamped his disappointment.

'Con, what are these holes doing in the floor?'

'For fresh air,' said Conor with a grin. 'When the whole contraption turns upside-down and traps you.'

Kate twitched, involuntarily, but Jem gave a superior smile, man to man. 'Go on! What *are* they for?'

'Save you from drowning when it rains.' Conor looked up at the sky. 'No fear of that today. This is the sort of day you dream about when you're shovelling muck in a hailstorm.'

The hissing of the engine suddenly built up to a fierce noise and, with a jerk and a creaking of carriages, the train started. Clouds of steam and smoke poured backwards over their heads and Jem heard for the first time the rattle of coaches over rails. He leaned out sideways, feeling the wind on his face and watching the blur of the houses rushing by. They drew out of Helmston almost immediately and began to travel along the coast. Grinning, Jem looked across at Kate, but she had no answering grin to give him. Her face was ash-pale.

'What's got you, Kate? Isn't it *glorious*!'

'Proper treat,' she said, hardly looking up and clutching the baby tightly on her lap.

Conor, who sat beside her, studied her carefully for a moment and then put one arm firmly about her shoulders. What he said to her Jem could not hear, but she smiled gratefully and did not shrink away.

In fifteen minutes they were there. It was the same distance, almost exactly, as had taken them three hours to walk from the village to Helmston. While Kate jumped, rather too eagerly, from the coach, Jem sat trying to work it all out.

'Come on now, lad, stir yourself,' Conor's voice broke in. 'You'll be missing the chance of seeing them load the rails for the main line.'

'The rails?' said Jem stupidly, only half come to himself.

'And wasn't that why they opened this branch first now? They were wanting to bring the rest of the stuff by sea and run it up the railway. It's a fine scheme. Why, the railways will put the carriers out of business, see if they don't.'

'Is there something the railways *can't* do?' asked Kate rather tartly as Conor led them across the yard. But he only smiled.

When they had seen the lengths of rail, new and gleaming, loaded on to their special trucks, they went off to find a place to eat their lunch. Kate refused point-blank to go inside the inn, so they sat on the harbour wall across the road with their bread and cheese, and Conor brought a jug of stout over from the inn.

The baby fared worst. Kate had brought her some milk in the bottle and some sop in a jar, but Martha was upset by the change in her placid life and she wriggled and screamed, until Conor took her on his knee and faced her out across the harbour.

'Take a look across there,' he said severely. 'Take a look at those rails coming off that fine little ship.'

Martha quietened miraculously and Kate glanced over her shoulder at the harbour. 'More rails?'

'They're landing all the rest of them,' said Conor, a touch of excitement in his voice. 'The work is going fine. There's only the tunnel to be finished now. When we meet in the middle of that, Miss Penfold, they can put down the last of the rails and open the line. By the end of April, they say.' He beamed at them as if he expected them to share his feelings. Kate managed a polite smile, but Jem was more straightforward.

'What's your plans? When it's finished?'

For a moment the Irishman looked strangely awkward, and then he said lightly, 'It's on to the next line and the next camp with me. I've not enough money saved yet.'

'For your cottage?' Kate said quickly, and he smiled at her.

'My cottage and my bit of land.' His eyes strayed out over the sea and he fell silent, until Kate roused him by taking Martha out of his arms. With a shake, like a dog coming out of water, he recovered himself.

'Will we take a turn round the harbour wall? Then there's the train to catch. We've a fair old walk back to the village.'

On the journey back, Kate approached the train with her chin up and her mouth set firm, but its terrors seemed to have faded for her. Conor pushed her firmly into a seat facing forwards, and within two minutes of starting she was pink and laughing in the wind, the ridiculous plumes on her bonnet waving and bobbing.

Her holiday mood held as they walked home. Jem had been dreading that part of the journey, expecting them all to be tired and quarrelsome, but their laughter carried them over the miles. It was a kind of release to Jem to see Kate so happy, for it meant he had no need to watch for one of her sour turns.

By the time they turned up the lane it was dark. Jem's feet were beginning to drag in spite of himself, and Martha slept against Conor's shoulder. As Kate paused to unlatch the cottage gate, Conor said teasingly, 'And isn't it a grand railway?'

'I still think folks do best to stay where God puts them,' Kate said firmly. But it was spirit, not temper, and she softened it at once with a smile. 'It was a good day, Mr O'Flynn. The best day I've had for years.'

Conor looked at her gravely over the gate. Softly he said, 'Kate Penfold, you're a lovely girl.'

She went scarlet with confusion and backed away, muttering that she must go inside first to light a candle. They heard her stumble into the unlit cottage and, for a moment or two, the sounds of her blundering movements came through the dark to them. Then a dot of flame broke the darkness.

And then they heard her scream.

CHAPTER NINE

Conor's dash for the cottage door sent Jem staggering into the hedge. He pulled himself out, taking no notice of the prickles, and followed as fast as he could. Kate was standing, quite still, in the middle of the cottage, a candlestick in her hand. Her whole body was totally rigid. As the others came in, she stayed motionless, saying nothing. Indeed, there was no point in saying anything. They could see only too clearly for themselves.

The whole place had been wrecked. Someone had pulled the dresser over on to its front in the middle of the floor and it lay surrounded by the wreckage of broken plates and of all the little jugs that Conor had bought. The cottage windows were smashed, and lumps of mud had been ground into the furniture and smeared over the walls and floor.

Conor looked at Kate. 'You'd do well to sit down a while. Will I make you a cup of tea?'

'No time to sit,' said Kate, in her cold, stiff voice. She pulled off her bright, new bonnet without a glance at it, took off her coat and handed both of them to Jem.

'Take those upstairs.'

'But, Kate, who could have——?'

'Who cares?' she said dully. 'It's no account. We must clear it, all the same.'

Jem looked at her, his eyes wide. 'Don't you want to know *why*?'

She shook her head wearily and stepped over to close the door, as if she would shut out the night and the rest of the world. As the door swung to, they all drew in their breath sharply. Nailed to the inside of the door, where they had not been able to see it before, was a paper. Kate and Jem stared at it without a word, until Conor said impatiently, 'What's it say? Tell me, for the love of heaven.'

Jem had not realized that Conor could not read. He opened his mouth to tell him what the paper said, but he could not make himself say the words, and in the end it was Kate who spoke the message aloud.

NO NAVVIES.

There was an awkward silence and, before Conor could break it, Kate had pulled herself together and was rattling out orders.

'Jem. Upstairs. Take the baby too. She'll likely sleep another hour or two. Mr O'Flynn. Would you be so good as to help me with the dresser?'

By the time Jem came downstairs again, the dresser was upright, the broken crockery and the worst of the mud swept into a pile in the centre of the cottage, and Kate and Conor were both on their knees washing the floor.

'More water,' Kate said without looking up. 'Put a pot on the fire to heat for the walls.'

Lugging the full black pot back from the well, Jem suddenly saw the scene like a picture. The End of The Holiday. This was how their special, carefree day had ended—him with a heavy pot of water and Kate and Conor scrubbing the floor in their best clothes. Kate must be very upset, he thought suddenly, to forget to change her clothes.

The sickness rose sour in his throat at the sight of the two of them, meekly on their knees because someone had decided to wreck their home. It was not right. Someone should fight back.

As the thought came into his head, he realized that he was the only person who could do it. Not Kate, with her desire to appear blameless and respectable. Not Conor, for he was not one of their family. He must do it himself. Without a word, he lugged the black pot the rest of the way across the floor, laid a fire and lit it. As soon as he had done that, he walked over to the door.

'Where you going?' Kate glanced up, damply wiping back a strand of hair.

'Out.' He slammed the door after him.

When he was outside the cottage, he found that he knew where to go. His feet led him almost automatically towards the forge. Not since the day when the fight was planned had he been inside, and now the taste of his fear and the memory of Joe's looming face came back to him, filling him with apprehension. But his desire to know was stronger. They would know all about it, some of those men grouped in front of the fire.

But when he got to the forge he found it cold and empty. It was one of the rare days when the men had not gathered, and although light came from the cottage at the side the forge fire was out and the door was shut. For a moment the warmth of relief flooded through him, and then he despised himself for shrinking. He forced himself to go closer to the forge and peer in at the windows. To check, he told himself. But it was really a test of his nerve. He was almost ready to imagine that the forge was full of men taking fierce oaths in the darkness.

But when he looked in at the window he could see nothing. He bent his head to set his ear to the keyhole.

All at once there was a rush and 'Got you!'

Shock made him hear it as a shout, made him sure that it was the blacksmith who had caught him. It was only after a second or two that he realized that the words had been hissed, not shouted, and that it was Ben who had spoken them.

'Ben! You gave me a proper fright.'

'Snooping!' Ben's voice was tight, shocking with hate. 'Looking for something to steal?'

'Great fool!' Jem's whisper was not as casual as he tried to make it. 'You ever seen me steal anything?'

'Huh!' said Ben scornfully, unable to disagree. 'What d'you want, then?'

'Looking for you.'

'Tell us another,' Ben said bitterly.

Jem felt himself begin to boil inwardly. It was Ben speaking like that. Ben! Gritting his teeth, he forced out the question he had come to ask.

'Who did it? Who did the cottage?'

Even through the darkness he could sense the smirk. 'Didn't like that, did you? I'll lay Kate didn't, either. Her precious clean cottage slobbered up with mud. That'll teach her to think herself a cut above other folks. She's nothing but navvy's trash.'

There was almost a sob in the defiance. Suddenly Jem realized that he was being taunted into a fight. As though to make certain, Ben hissed at him again.

'She's not *good* enough for Elijah Day!'

That hurt. Having their friendly joke used against him. Jem sighed inwardly. He did not want to fight Ben. Where was the use in that? Ben alone had not done what was done to the cottage, and he could not have planned it. Nevertheless, Jem found himself pulling off his smock and rolling up his sleeves. As he turned to face Ben and squared up, the other boy said, as a final taunt, 'I broke the first window.'

At that, Jem saw nothing but whirling wheels of fury and he plunged in, his fists thudding.

They had often fought before, rolling about for fun as much as anything else, but as soon as Jem's head had cleared enough for him to think at all he became aware that this was different. Ben was normally a cautious fighter but now he lashed out, careless of his own safety, concerned for nothing but hitting and hurting. Blow after blow caught Jem, stinging his ears and pounding his stomach, and at first he could not hit back hard enough. He could not forget that this was Ben, who had been his friend all his life, Ben whom he had missed so badly all these months.

But as his ears grew sore and his arms ached from parrying, fury took over again and he became unthinking, hitting back blow for blow.

They fell to the ground, giving up any pretence at fighting by rules, pulling and clawing, battering and grinding into the mud, until Jem came to and found himself sitting astride his opponent, panting as he looked down. They were below the window of the cottage and, in the faint light, he could see Ben's face, frightened and contorted. Still hot from the fight, he almost smashed his fist straight down on to it. Enemy face. But it wasn't. It was Ben. He drew a deep breath.

'Tell me. Who did it?'

Ben looked up, his mouth open, breathing noisily. Then he began to gasp out names and Jem shrivelled inside. People he had known all his life. Boys he had played with and men he had looked up to. Choking stopped his throat and the longing to get up and go away nearly overcame him. But the job had to be finished. He forced the words out.

'Whose idea was it?'

Unmistakably, defeated and flat on his back as he was, Ben looked proud.

'My dad. It was his idea.'

Now, thought Jem. Now I should take a stone and smash it in his face. But his arms felt heavy and unwilling.

'*Why?* What've we done to you?'

Ben's lips drew back in a grimace. 'Navvy-lovers! That's what you are. And your sister prancing down the road in a tart's bonnet. And the fight.'

'The fight? Your dad lost fair and square.'

'You set it up! You set my dad up and that navvy of yours beat him with a dirty Irish trick.'

Instinctively Jem's right hand went out for a stone to beat the lie away from Ben's mouth. But as his fingers groped in the mud they met not stone but metal. He pulled it up. It was a cart-horse's shoe. The sort he and Ben had used in their games of quoits. For a moment he stared at it as his anger loosened and grew cold, and then he looked back to Ben's scared and twisted face. With a sad, contemptuous movement, he dropped the heavy shoe on to Ben's chest and let go of him.

The other boy did not move. Only his eyes flicked. 'You off? Going to get your navvy friend to beat up my dad? Has he got many more dirty tricks?'

Jem looked down for a moment. Then, silently, he rose to his feet, pulled on his smock and made for the gate, hardly hearing the taunt, 'Navvy-lover!', that Ben flung after him.

He felt nothing. Blank. He had struck a blow, but it had brought him no joy. He had got the names he wanted, but what was he going to do with them? More fights? More tight, twisted hatred? That was not what he wanted. What he wanted—and as he thought it he saw that it was impossible—was Ben and Conor, both, for his friends.

Chapter Ten

It was a bitter spring that came to the Penfolds in the silent village, as they moved automatically from task to task. Now it was they who cut themselves off from their neighbours. Either satisfied or ashamed of themselves, the other villagers showed signs of wanting to pretend that nothing had happened, but their friendly overtures were met with blankness. Jem found himself turning his head and casting his eyes down when he was faced by George Pearce, Ted Funnell, or any one of a dozen others. However much their faces smiled, all he could see was their hands. He saw those hands pulling the dresser, breaking the windows, smearing the mud. Wreckers' hands. The thought of it stood between him and all the other people in the village. Even Hoppy Noyce, who had had no part in the wrecking. Even fat, foolish Elijah Day. They were all Village.

Nor was there any more warmth at home. Anyone who looked in casually might have thought that things in the cottage had been put right. Kate had scrubbed and scoured for a whole week, her red elbows jerking furiously, and Conor had made a special trip to Helmston for new glass and lead, paying for them himself, so that the windows need not be stuffed with rags. The bones of the cottage were mended. But the heart had gone out of it. There were no more friendly evenings of talk and stories. Kate never sang and Conor left early for the line and came home late. The navvies were blasting a tunnel through the Downs at Crayston—the last big piece of work to be done on

111

the line—and Conor staggered in exhausted every night.
After hours of extra work, he was ready for nothing
except food and sleep. The three of them lived separate
lives, moving wordlessly like figures in a dance. It was as
though they had been put under an enchantment of
speechlessness and had no will to break it. They could
not bring themselves to talk about what had happened
and, not being able to talk about that, they could not
talk about anything else. Even Miss Ellen, who came
round shyly to offer help, was sent away coldly and
almost rudely by Kate. And, all the time, Jem could feel
everything in the village and at home coiling up tighter
and tighter.

It was three weeks after the wrecking that he woke
suddenly in the night. For a moment, half-asleep, he lay
wary with fright at the black shape which loomed over
him, its breath noisy in the silence. Then he realized
that it was the Irishman come late to bed.

'Con!' he whispered.

'Hush it now. You'll have the whole village in here.
You be off to sleep.'

'Where've you been?'

Conor sat down on the edge of the bed to take off his
boots. 'I've just come from dining with Her Majesty.
Sure, it's terrible late hours she keeps.'

'*Conor!*' Jem sat up. 'Were you drinking up at the
camp?'

'There's more to the world than drink.' Conor sighed.
'If you can keep your tongue to yourself . . . well . . . I
was up on the Beacon.'

'In the dark?'

'It's a grand place for thinking.'

The bed jerked as he pulled at his boots.

'You could think here,' Jem said, rather shyly. Conor
turned to face him in the dark.

'Listen, lad. Have you, maybe, been thinking I was unfriendly, these last few weeks?'

Jem nodded, ridiculously, as though Conor could see him.

'I was half afraid you would.' The Irishman took silence for consent. 'But I must keep out from under your sister's feet.'

'Why?'

'Well . . . if she keeps catching sight of me, now, wouldn't she be remembering that she wants me out of the house for good?'

'But she *likes* you.'

'Liked, may be.' The old, wooden frame creaked as Conor climbed into bed. 'Likes is different.'

'Aw, *you've* not done anything.'

'Not what I've done, boy. What I am. I'm the man that gets her windows broken for her, turns her neighbours from speaking to her.' It was said bitterly, as Jem had never heard him speak before.

'But she wouldn't,' he whispered quickly. 'Not for no fault of yours. She wouldn't turn you out.'

'Maybe,' the Irishman said slowly, as if the idea were painful in his mind, 'maybe if I was a decent man I'd pack my bags and be off without waiting for the asking.'

'But you can't!' hissed Jem desperately. 'You can't up and leave us. Not now.'

'Don't I know it. I can't go and I can't stay. What's to be done?'

'You could—' Jem rummaged in his mind. It was dull with sleep and it took him a second or two to see the answer. 'You could take us along. Like your family.'

'You mean,' Conor said, very softly and slowly, 'you mean I should marry your sister?'

'Oh *no!*' Jem's embarrassment made him squeak. 'I'm sorry. I wasn't thinking. I never meant—' The way she

113

was now, he thought miserably, probably not even Elijah Day would have her.

The bed began to shake in a strange way and Jem was bewildered until he realized that it was Conor, laughing noiselessly. Laughing as though Jem had said something ridiculous beyond words.

'Con?'

'Sure,' he gasped, 'sure and you're younger than I thought.' But it was said kindly. 'Do you think I'd not ask her tomorrow if I thought she'd have me?'

'*Kate?*' It was like being knocked down a flight of stairs.

Conor chuckled. 'Wasn't I the same about my sister? A fat, foul-mouthed colleen, she was to my eyes. And half the men in the village courting her. It's a strange business.'

But Jem was in no mind for jokes. 'Kate? You'd marry Kate?'

'Ssshhh! Remember that wall's thin. Haven't I just said I would?'

'You'd marry her and go off?' Jem's mind was whirling, a crazy hope seeping in. Conor began to talk softly.

'If I'd my stocking full, I'd take the three of you off to Ireland tomorrow and we'd be a farmer and his family before you could turn round.' He sighed. 'But it's another five years at least, to my reckoning, before I'll have enough saved, and your sister married and mother long before.'

'Ask her.' Jem's tongue nearly twisted itself, eager as he was to snatch this chance. 'Ask her *now*. She likes you. We could come up to the camp and keep house for you. Ask her now.'

'A fine idea,' said the Irishman dryly. 'She'd like well to be woken in the night with an offer of a navvy life.'

Jem was actually shivering with impatience, and in his earnestness he found the right words. 'Do you think she wants to stay here? Do you think we want to stay in the village?'

There was a long pause. At last Conor heaved himself over, turning his back to Jem. 'We'll see. In the morning, maybe. Now, off to sleep with you.' And he made as though he were sleeping, but Jem, lying awake almost until dawn, could tell from his breathing that it was not so.

Next morning, the whole thing seemed dreamlike. Conor was gone before Jem woke, and Kate was as crabbed as ever. But, in spite of that, it seemed to Jem that what he had planned was sure to come true. Conor would marry Kate and they would all escape to the line. He had his first day's work for weeks and, as he strode across the field, dibbling behind Hoppy Noyce, he tried to push the midnight whispers to the back of his mind. But his face gave him away. It smiled uncontrollably. Hoppy Noyce, bent and crabbed with rheumatism, grumbled his way round the field with the dibber and Jem followed, dropping beans and smiling. When they stopped for breakfast, Hoppy grunted at him, 'Pleased to have a bit of work again, are you?'

'Doesn't come amiss,' Jem said, biting into his raw onion.

'Hmmph.' Hoppy was always gloomy, but that was just his way, Jem knew. He had a kind heart. His gaze now was almost pitying. 'Seems you'll soon be needing all the work you can get. Come the end of April.'

'Oh?' Jem stared at him, chewing onion. 'Why April?'

'What's wrong with your ears, then? Full of mud? Everyone's heard it. Those navvies of yours have to be done with the line by the end of April, else they'll lose their bonuses. As if they didn't have enough money to

115

fling about already.' He spat scornfully into the hedge. 'That's why they've been at it day and night these last weeks, finishing their precious tunnel up at Crayston.'

'Ah.' Jem tried to look solemn, and Hoppy patted his knee.

'I'll put in a word for you with farmer. See if he can't come by a bit of extra work.'

It was difficult to look properly grateful. By the end of April it wouldn't matter. By the end of April, he and Kate and Martha would not even be in the village any more. To hide the grin that was spreading over his face, Jem stood up and turned his back on Hoppy to chuck his onion over the hedge. As it landed, square in the puddle he was aiming at, he saw Ben coming up the lane.

'Hallo, Ben!' In his cheerfulness, he forgot that they had last met with their fists. 'Where're you off to, then?'

Ben stopped with a jerk and turned a bright, hot red. 'Nowhere . . . I . . . none of your business, is it then!'

He walked on at twice the speed. For a moment, Jem stopped smiling, amazed that Ben could hate him so much that he could not even speak. But before he could sort it out in his mind, Hoppy Noyce was shaking his shoulder.

'Come on, lad. Beans won't sow themselves, and there's this whole field to finish by dusk.'

Still bewildered, Jem turned to follow Hoppy up the next row, dropping the beans four to a hole as he had been taught.

> One for the mouse and one for the crow,
> One to rot and one to grow

There was no sense in thinking about Ben. Come the end of April and he would probably never see him again.

116

The field stretched ahead of him, wide and open, like the path which would lead him away from the village. For, surely, Conor would not change his mind. Ben did not matter.

But it was not so easy to forget about him. At the end of the day, Jem left Hoppy knocking mud off his boots in the far corner of the field and ran for the gate, eager to get home and see if Conor had spoken yet. As he dashed through, he all but knocked into two people coming down the lane. One of them was Ben and the other was someone he had never seen before, a thin-lipped man with a sour, yellowish skin, who was wearing a jacket instead of a smock.

'Hallo!' Jem said breathlessly. He could hardly avoid it, nearly having bumped them.

'Hallo.' Ben would have walked straight on, but Jem looked towards his companion expectantly.

'Friend of yours?' A stranger was not such a usual sight that you let him pass by without a comment.

'Mother's cousin Walt, from up Stanning way,' muttered Ben.

The stranger smiled at Jem, a cold, ingratiating smile. 'Young Ben here's just been taking me for a walk up by Crayston. To look at the railway tunnel and—'

Quite suddenly, he stopped, and Jem let the two of them go without another word, amazed. He had quite distinctly seen Ben kick his grown-up cousin on the leg as soon as he mentioned Crayston tunnel. And, instead of giving him a cuff on the ear, the cousin had obediently stopped talking. But why? Jem puzzled over it as he walked on. Folks were always going to look at the tunnel, and no wonder. A fine sight it was, with towers like a castle at the end of it. Even those who hated the railway had been known to sneak off for a glimpse of it. Altogether, Ben was behaving very strangely.

But as he came alongside the gate, everything to do with Ben went out of his head. Conor and Kate were together at the cottage door, and Jem shrank behind the hedge, not wanting to disturb them before Conor had had his say. Very slowly, Kate raised her hand and laid it on the Irishman's sleeve, and he covered it with his own. Jem let out his breath. It must be done. They could all leave. They were free.

But, the next moment, Conor bent down and picked up his old leather bag, his bundle and his tools, which had been lying hidden just inside the cottage door. With a nod at Kate, he made off down the path, while she stood in the doorway, shading her eyes to watch him.

'Con!' Jem met him at the gate. 'What is it?'

Conor smiled wryly. 'What do you think?'

'But ask her. Ask her and it will be all right!'

'No, lad.' Conor's voice was tired. 'That was bad advice you gave me last night, and it's a fool I was to take it.'

Before he had finished speaking, he was on his way down the lane, with none of the usual spring in his step, and Jem looked after him, open-mouthed, too amazed even to think of saying goodbye. That Kate would refuse his offer—that Kate would refuse any offer—simply had not occurred to him and he was stunned. Then, coming to life, he stormed through the gate and into the cottage, dizzy with fury. Kate sat at the table, eerily still, studying the backs of her hands.

'You sour old maid!' The words poured out. 'What've you done? Do you think anyone will ever ask you again? What did you think you were doing, turning him down?'

'What I had to do,' she said dully, not looking up.

'We could have gone. We could have got away. And you've spoilt it all.'

'Gone to what?' She looked at him scornfully. 'The camp? Five years of that, or more, it would be.'

'But they can't be so bad. You've not even looked.'

She glanced down at her hands again and muttered, 'There was a woman attacked today. Over Little Morden way. They doubt she'll live.'

Jem stared at her, still gripped by anger. 'You're afraid. You've sent him away because you're a coward.'

Suddenly her stillness broke, and she jumped up, hammering the table with her fist. '*I've* spoilt it? You great ninny. Do you think I wouldn't go up there now, if it was only me? It's you and Martha. I can't take you to grow up there.'

'Me?' A choking came up in Jem's throat so that he could say no more. The thing he most wanted in the world. The place he most wanted to go. And here he was, being protected from it, because he was too young. It seemed madness. And yet he was honest enough with himself to see that Kate had lost far more than he had, and she was masking her disappointment with anger. But he was sick with sadness, and he could not tell her he was sorry. The whole thing was too important for politeness. He turned and stumbled out of the cottage, knocking himself on the door-frame as he went. Half-running, half-walking he passed the bakehouse, the forge, the Rectory, and stormed out of the village as far as the Copse. There, he and Ben had an old hiding place. He wriggled into the middle of the bush and, when the thick branches over the hollow hid him, he cried until he was exhausted.

When his eyes were dry again, he lay for a while without moving, but the wind was cold and the earth was colder and they forced him at last to crawl out and set off back to the village. He was reluctant to go home, but the night was overcast and soon it would be hard to see one step in front of the other. It was no night for wandering the Beacon. He started to walk back slowly, spinning out the journey.

Half-way into the village, he saw George Pearce and Ted Funnell ahead of him, making for the forge. Vaguely, his mind still taken up with other things, he thought that there was something unusual about the way that they were walking. It was not their customary slow amble, drifting along for a chat after supper and pausing at every other door to ask after someone or crack a joke. Tonight, they were striding out purposefully, not looking to one side or the other. Jem kept his distance behind them. He did not feel like talking to anyone from the village.

But as he came round the corner to the forge, following them, he suddenly began to pay proper attention. For the lanes which led up the crossroads at the forge were all full of men, and all the men were walking with the same grim determination as Ted and George. No one took any notice of Jem, but he saw Hoppy Noyce stopped outside the forge and he went forward and caught at his sleeve.

'What's up, Mr Noyce? What's happened?'

Hoppy shook his head at him sadly. 'Mud in your ears again, boy? Surely you've heard? A navvy set on a woman up Little Morden way and—'

'And that navvy lodger of yours had best watch out!' broke in Ted Funnell, who was leaning against the railings. 'We don't want the like of him here.'

'You needn't worry about him,' Jem said bitterly. 'He's gone.'

'Best way,' Ted said shortly. 'They're all the same, those navvies. If that woman dies—'

'They've not caught the man yet?' Hoppy said, trying to soothe him down.

'No, nor ever will. That scum! They'd hide each other from God himself.'

The other men, passing behind him into the forge, rumbled their agreement, and one or two of them spat at Jem's feet as they went by him. Hoppy put an arm across Jem's shoulders.

'It's not the lad's fault. And you'll do yourself no good raging, Ted Funnell. There's still only forty-odd of us to a thousand of them. There's nothing to be done.'

Slowly and ominously, Ted Funnell levered himself away from the railings. 'We'll see about that now, won't we. Joe's got something in his mind for sure. He's not the man to call us all together like this to play crown and anchor, is he? And I'm with him whatever it is. Just so long as it's strong enough.'

With a frown at Jem, he joined the stream of men squeezing into the small forge. Looking after him, Jem could see that almost everyone was there. Across the far side, in the half-dark he could even see the rough cloth of a jacket. Mrs Hamage's cousin Walt. Even he was there. Jem took a step towards the door. Perhaps he could slide quietly into a corner and listen to what was up. But, even as he moved, he saw Hoppy shake his head. There was no place for him in there. Even though Con had gone, the village had not forgiven the Penfolds. Jem stood and watched Hoppy follow the last of the men through the doorway and listened to the thud of the door as it shut in his face, cutting him off from everyone else. He was so miserable that he did not stop to wonder why the door, which always stood open, should be shut on a warm, close evening with the place cramful of people. Dragging his feet, he went the rest of the way back to the cottage.

As he entered, Kate almost flung herself on him, pulling him right inside.

'Where've you been? I've been half out of my mind with worry. There's such a mood in the village tonight—'

'Leave me go,' he said, shaking her arm off. He still had not forgiven her. 'I'm not a baby.'

'You've got no more sense than one. The men are wild with rage about that poor woman. It's no night for you to be out. Didn't you see them?'

'I met them all going up to the forge.' Jem sat down. 'Joe Hamage called them together. Got some notion in his head.'

'He's always got some notion in his head,' Kate said wearily. 'What is it this time?'

'How should I know?' He almost shouted it at her in his bitterness. 'There's no place for me at the forge, is there? They're not going to take us back into the village just because you've sent Conor away. A fine mess you've made. We don't belong anywhere any more.'

'It had to be done.' Kate was obstinate. 'And you're better out of the forge tonight with the anger that's about in the village. You don't want to get snarled up with Joe Hamage's notions.'

'That's all you care about, isn't it? Staying respectable? You'll be the most respectable old maid in the county,' he said cruelly, beginning to unlace his boots. '*You* didn't have to stand by while they took in a stranger and shut the forge door in your face!'

'Stranger? What stranger?' But she did not sound really interested.

'Some cousin of Ben's mother. Walt, his name was.'

'Ah, Walt Cooper that'll be. What's he want? Thought he was too grand to come visiting here ever since he started work up Stanning Quarry.'

'Been up to Crayston with Ben. To take a look at the tunnel.'

'That doesn't sound like Walt. He was never a one for admiring another man's work. I remember him when I was a little girl. A slimy, creeping creature he was. Is he still the same?'

Jem shrugged. He was not so angry now, but he had no mind to sit chatting to Kate. He'd get his boots off and go to bed. What did he care if some quarryman had been up to Crayston tunnel? Some quarryman . . . the idea hit him so hard that it made him breathless for a moment. He stopped moving, with his fingers on the laces of his second boot, and thought back over the queer things that had happened that day. The odd way Ben had acted. The men trooping grimly into the forge to hear Joe Hamage's notion. The speed with which Walt Cooper had stopped talking when Ben kicked him on the ankle. Without looking up, he said, in a tight voice, 'What does he do up Stanning Quarry then? That Walt?'

'I dunno. Sets the charges, I think,' Kate said casually. 'He—'

All of a sudden she went totally white and put a hand on the table to steady herself. 'Oh, Jem,' she whispered, 'they never would.'

For a moment they stared at each other, unable to speak. Then Kate shook her head in a dazed way. 'Come on, lad. We must be turning daft. They *never* would.'

But now that the idea had come to her as well Jem felt more certain of it. 'That tunnel'd blow well,' he said thoughtfully, 'for a man that knew where to set the charges.'

'But where's the point?' Kate rubbed her hand across her forehead and sat down with a thump. 'If they blow up the tunnel, that won't hurt the navvies. It'll just keep them here longer. It doesn't make sense.'

'But it will hurt the navvies.' Jem was remembering what Hoppy Noyce had told him. 'They must finish come the end of April, or they lose money.' He looked at Kate's reddened hands clasping and unclasping themselves on the table-top and felt how alone the two of them were. 'That's Joe's plan for certain. If you'd seen Ben today. He was that queer—but what can we *do*, Kate? We don't even know when it's to be.'

'It's tonight!' She began to speak quickly, the words flooding out. 'It must be. There's no moon tonight, and Joe Hamage is a clever man. He'll talk them into madness and not leave them time to go off and think about it. Oh, the *fools*! There'll be blood and more blood, and all to save Joe Hamage's precious pride.'

'But what can we do?' Jem said again.

For a moment he thought she was as lost as he was. Helplessly she glanced round the room, like a child looking for someone to come to her aid. Then she seemed to pull herself together. Staring straight into his eyes, she said with determination, 'Off with you then. Get Conor.'

'Con? But—'

'Aw, don't be such a *child*!' She came round the table and pulled him to his feet. 'Con must be told and you are the one to do it. He'll be up at the camp, and I can't go there.'

'But what if we're wrong? Or if Joe does not get them to do it?'

'You've seen the temper the men were in,' Kate said scornfully. 'Do you think they'd refuse a chance like that?'

124

Jem knew that she was right. And, all of a sudden, he was certain. The village men were plotting to blow up Crayston tunnel. That night. He began to pull on his boots.

'Tell Con,' Kate said breathlessly, 'and tell no one else. Oh, Jem, get him! Get him!'

Tying the last lace, Jem shot out of the cottage, leaving Kate gazing after him. He crept carefully through the main part of the village and, when he came to the forge, stopped a minute and tried to peer through the small window, grey with dirt. He did not dare to stop for more than a second, but he had time to see grim faces round the forge, their eyes fixed on the quarryman, and what he saw sent him scurrying up the Beacon towards the navvy camp, his hands and feet scrabbling at the turf.

CHAPTER ELEVEN

In his hurry, he stumbled right into the middle of the camp before he had time to think what he was doing. He staggered to a halt, not knowing how to start looking for Conor. The camp was much bigger than it looked from far away. The dark shapes of the huts stood up on every side, some large, some small, some black and shuttered and some with open doors, across which shadowy figures moved against the light of the fires. It was as big as the village at least, and much busier. Panting, Jem stood still and stared around, bewildered, while small children bumped him and mangy dogs sniffed his ankles. Then a navvy passed close to him and Jem grabbed at his sleeve.

'Here!' The man turned, fierce, and shook off his hand.

'Please, I—'

'What are you after?'

'I'm looking for Mr—for Kilkenny Con.'

'Kilkenny?' The man laughed thickly. 'You won't find him up here. Got some woman down in the village. Crafty devil.'

The man lurched off, and Jem looked around desperately. To his relief, he suddenly caught sight of Ginger and he crossed the space between them before he had time to catch a breath.

'Ginger!'

'What? Oh, hallo, young shaver. What's up with you, then?'

'Con. I must find Con.'

'He not down at your place then?' said Ginger

conversationally, as if there were all the time in the world.

'No. And I *must* find him!'

'No accounting for tastes. Well, if he's here he'll be up at Fat Maggie's. Last hut on the right over there. Want me to come along?'

But Jem had already shot away. 'Mind she don't bounce on you,' Ginger shouted after him with a grin.

Fat Maggie's was big, but it was more of a hovel than most. Jem paused at the doorway, looking for somewhere to knock, but the walls were made of earth and the roof and door of tarpaulins. Bending his head, he went in under the looped-up door and was blinded for a moment by the darkness, unable to see anything but the red glow of the fire.

'Yes? What do you want?' It snapped at him out of the dark.

'Kilkenny Con,' he said towards where the voice had come from. 'I want Kilkenny.'

A vast lump of blackness moved against the light of the fire, silently.

'Please do you know where he is?' Jem said desperately. 'I want him.'

Out of the black shape came a wheeze, like someone bouncing on a creaky chair. 'You must be the only one as does,' said the voice in tones of great amusement. 'But he's here all right.'

Jem looked around, but he could see nothing away from the light of the fire. Suddenly, the doorway erupted in a flood of noise and lanterns as ten or twelve navvies surged through.

'Sitting in the dark, Maggie? Mean old cow you are.'

'Where's my grub, then? Bet you've eaten it all yourself, you old lard-barrel.'

'God save us, Maggie! The smell! You must be the worst cook in Sussex.'

Jem could see Maggie now. She was not in the least put out by the insults that came at her, but stood with her arms folded, looking at the men. Her enormous body blocked out nearly all the heat from the fire and her chins rippled down over her chest. She was dressed in a sacking skirt and a man's jacket, and the sweat ran off her like a waterfall.

Jem would have liked to ask her again where Con was, for although he had looked about in the flickering lantern-light he could not see him. But Maggie was surrounded by navvies clamouring for their dinners, and Jem was forced to wait.

'Nothing wrong with your dinners,' Maggie shouted above the hubbub. 'Get and eat them.'

She moved so that the men could reach the fire and they clustered round the big black pot. Out of the pot came a dozen strings with notched sticks on the end, and each man searched, pushing and shoving, until he found his own stick. Then they all took the sticks and wound up the string, pulling nets out of the pot. Each man had his own dinner cooked in his own net. Maggie stood by with a huge wooden spoon, banging the fingers of anyone who tried to sneak a bit of his neighbour's food.

'And keep your pickers off that,' she said, pointing to the last stick. 'I put them potatoes in for Kilkenny.'

One of the men laughed. 'Think he'll care? Not the way *he* is.'

The mention of Kilkenny had reminded Maggie of Jem and, looking up, she saw him still standing there.

'Don't gape at me. If you want him, go and get him. He's down there.' She laughed creakily again as she pointed with her spoon-handle.

128

Following with his eyes, Jem saw what he had not noticed before. On one of the bunks at the other end of the hut was a dark shape. When he had taken a couple of steps down the hut, he could see that it was Conor and that he was asleep. Jem stood over him and shook him. Then he realized that the Irishman was very fast asleep. His mouth dropped open and his breathing sounded thick. Jem shook again, but Conor only moved his head slightly.

'Maggie,' Jem shouted, not knowing what else to call her, 'is he all right?'

Maggie laughed in great gulps, as if he had made a fine joke, but she came down the hut towards him.

'Never seen a drunken man before?'

'Drunk?' It had not occurred to Jem. With a sinking of despair, he said it again. 'Drunk?'

Maggie shoved him impatiently. 'And why not? He's not turned parson has he? Or Methodee? Come in hours ago, as black as a stormy Monday. "What's up?" I says. "You dropped your dinner and found a walnut?" "Something like that," he says. So I told him to go off and get drunk. Best thing.'

'And he did?' Jem did not know what to do if Conor could not be roused.

'Not exactly. Made a stab at it, but he got on the wrong side of Pigtail. Can't stand drinking with a gloomy man, can't Pigtail. So he nips round behind him and knocks him over the head with a bottle.' She slapped Con's shoulder affectionately. 'Silly old fool!'

'But Maggie, I've got to talk to him!'

'Talk away. He won't take offence.'

'I *must*.'

She looked at him shrewdly. 'You trying to put one over on me?'

'No. Honest.'

She went on looking for a moment and then nodded briskly. 'I'll get him on his feet for you. But it'd better be good. They don't like being messed with. I could show you the bruises to prove it.'

But, instead, she waddled off down the hut to where the other men were cramming in their dinners, taking no notice of Jem.

'Redhead. Saucepan. Get us a couple of buckets of water.'

'Give over, Mag.' But they went. They brought the buckets of water down to the bed end of the hut and stood to watch what she would do. She picked up each bucket in turn and, with no regard for Con's clothes or the bed, emptied it over his head. The first bucketful only set him stirring, but at the second bucketful he opened his eyes, groaned and swore. Maggie looked at him with satisfaction. 'He'll do. Roll him off the bed.'

Saucepan and Redhead looked at each other with a shrug and did as she said. The shock of hitting the floor woke Conor properly.

'On your feet, Kilkenny.' Maggie reached a hand down and pulled him up.

'Get off, Mag.' He shoved her away and then winced and put a hand to his head. 'I never drank *that* much?'

She grinned at him. 'More Pigtail than gin. He didn't fancy your moaning, so he put one on you.'

Jem was watching anxiously. Seeing Conor's eyes fixed open, he burst out—'Con, you must—' but Maggie's push sent him staggering.

'Give over. It can wait till he's had a mouthful of food.'

Conor looked as though the last thing he wanted was food, but she ignored that and pushed him over to the other end of the hut. As he slumped on to a chair and groaned again, she slapped a plateful of potatoes down in front of him.

'Get that down you. And bring your own tomorrow. This isn't the Union.'

The other men jeered at him while he ate.

'Better now, Kilkenny?'

'Thought you could hold your drink.'

'What did Pigtail do? Hit you with his pegleg?'

Conor ate stolidly, ignoring everything, and by the time he had finished the plateful he looked a deal better. There was even a touch of jauntiness in the way he turned to Maggie.

'What is it then, Mag? It'd better be good, now.'

She shrugged, a huge lifting of her shoulders that almost buried her head in fat.

'Ask the boy.'

Conor looked round, still rather muzzy. When he caught sight of Jem he almost fell off his chair.

'And what are *you* doing here?'

'Kate—' began Jem. And then stuck.

Conor looked at him gravely. 'It's in my mind that we'd best not talk about that.'

'No—not that. She wants your help. That is—' He was beginning to get confused about who needed help, and the whole problem suddenly burst out with no more ceremony.

'The village men are going to blow up Crayston tunnel.'

'WHAT?' It came not just from Conor but from all the rest of the men in the hut. They pressed closer and, too late, Jem remembered that Kate had told him to tell no one but Conor. Well, what could it matter? He hurried on, trying to explain.

'They've got a quarryman from over Stanning way. To set the charges.'

The men growled amongst themselves, and more and more pressed into the hut, called in as they passed.

Conor kept his eyes on Jem's face. 'And why would they want to do that, now?'

'Revenge. For the woman. The one that might die.'

Conor looked even graver. 'She's dead. Shame on him that did it and those that are hiding him.'

'What is that to us?' It was Pigtail, breaking through the crowd. His face was fierce in the firelight. 'We are not the man who was killing the stupid creature.'

Jem cowered away from the fierceness, but Pigtail leaned closer. 'And is this true? Not a trickery?'

'Yes. Yes, it's true,' babbled Jem. He prayed that he was right.

Pigtail held up a hand behind him for silence and, when he had it, snapped out one word.

'When?'

Jem was mesmerized by the black eyes. 'Tonight.'

Anything else he might have said was drowned in a roar as the navvies dashed from the hut. When they had all gone, all but Conor, Jem and Maggie, Conor looked at Jem and shook his head ruefully.

'A fine pickle you've landed us in. It's like tinder they are, and they'll fire the rest of the camp.'

Jem realized at last the wisdom of Kate's advice. Perhaps Conor could have dealt with things more quietly.

'I'm sorry.'

Maggie thumped Conor on the back. 'Give over jawing the lad. Get out there and do something to stop them.'

Conor jumped up. 'Maggie, you may be fat, but you've twice the sense of any other woman to match it, and it's myself would marry you if I were three times the size.'

She snorted and pushed him outside, and outside the scene was enough to wipe the jokes from anyone's lips. Pigtail, standing on a barrel in the middle of the camp, was rousing the navvies, who crowded round him in a vast rabble, hundreds strong. Each time he shouted something, he emphasized it by banging his wooden leg on the barrel and the crowd howled approval.

'They're near ready to go,' Conor said into Jem's ear. 'We must do what we can to turn them aside. Hang on to me.'

He gripped Jem's wrist and pulled him hurly-burly through the crowd to the foot of the barrel. There, he got the other navvies to lift him up so that he could whisper in Pigtail's ear. The men hushed again, to hear what was going on.

'Is good!' Pigtail shouted when Conor had finished. 'It will stop escaping. Kilkenny will take some of you and talk with these villagers at their end of the tunnel. The rest—with me! We will come up the tunnel and take them from behind.'

On the roar of approval, he clambered down from the barrel and set off towards the south end of the tunnel, hobbling over the Beacon at twice the walking speed of an ordinary man. Men streamed after him, strung out like some unruly procession, torches flaming in their hands. Conor poked Jem in the back.

'Stop your gaping, lad. We must be at the front.'

'What for?' panted Jem, as he was hauled through the crowd of men making for the north end of the tunnel.

'Don't be a fool!' Conor said sharply. But as they got to the front of the crowd he explained. 'There'll be murder done if we're not there first. And like as not if we do. Still, the worst ones have gone with Pigtail, and that gives us a bit of time.'

'But don't you want to fight? It's *Joe*. Let them fight him.' Jem felt venomous.

Conor caught at his shoulder and pulled him along faster, speaking without turning his head sideways, as if he grudged the waste of breath.

'I'll fight that one myself when I want him fought. Gladly. But do you think these will stop at that? Once their blood is up?'

At last Jem realized, with a cold clenching in his stomach. 'You mean—they might attack the village?'

Conor strode on, his face stern, not bothering to reply.

'But what'll we do?'

A faint, wry smile twitched the corner of the Irishman's mouth. 'You pray a Protestant prayer, lad, and I'll pray a Catholic prayer, if I can remember one. Maybe He'll have the decency to listen to one of us.'

He loped over the Beacon, Jem half-running to keep up with him, while behind them and off to their left the lines of torches snaked through the darkness and the chant of the men who carried them beat in the night like the tramp of feet.

'Cray-ston. Cray-ston. Cray-ston.'

Chapter Twelve

When they came to the edge of the Beacon, Conor and Jem were well ahead and they paused at the slope to look down towards the tunnel. Despite himself, Jem found his head flung back excitedly and his body pulsing in time to the march, as if he were taking part in some carnival. The mood of the men behind had infected him and as he and Conor looked down he said, without thinking, 'But they'll have fair warning if they're there already.'

'Of course,' Conor said calmly, pushing him on down the slope, on to the road.

'But they'll make off!'

For a while Conor did not reply, as they hurried down the hillside. At the bottom of the hill, the road took a sharp left turn, on to the bridge over the new railway line. Here Conor stopped and leaned on the parapet.

'Listen. What is it that you want? To save the tunnel?'

'Yes. But—'

'But you want them punished?'

'Ye-es.' Suddenly Jem was not so sure. It had been a grand thing to march with the navvies, but now, as they came up behind, fierce and noisy, he could see why the villagers feared and hated them.

Conor pressed his advantage home. 'It's your own folk we're going against.'

That was true. Ben's father. Ted the ploughman. George, the tallest man in the village. The people he had known all his life. Suddenly the whole thing seemed incredible. He and Kate must be wrong.

'Suppose—' he began, with a quick pinch of fear, 'suppose—'

But Conor had stopped listening. With a frown on his face he was gazing up the dark cutting towards the tunnel.

'The fools! The stupid fools!'

'What?' Jem leant over the side of the bridge and strained his eyes to see as Conor flapped his hand at the black half-circle of the tunnel-mouth. It was lit up now, faintly, by the flames of the torches as the navvies streamed down the hillside and on to the bridge. Dimly, Jem could see what had caught Conor's eye. Shapes moving. Human figures. And they showed no signs of flight. Instead, they were ranging themselves in a line across the mouth of the tunnel.

The navvies crowded on to the bridge, following Conor, and then began to slither down the sides of the cutting. But as they came near the cutting floor a dark figure approached from the tunnel-mouth waving a lantern.

'Wait!'

It was Joe. He bellowed hugely, and then paused until the noise of the navvies was all but silenced, as they stopped, taken by surprise. Half of them were still on the bridge and the others were scattered down the slopes so that the torches made a semi-circle of guttering light in which the isolated figure of the smith stood out as if he were on a stage. He walked up the cutting until he was midway between the tunnel and the bridge and then began to shout, very slowly, with his head flung back.

'The charges are laid!'

The silence was complete now, and he gazed round in satisfaction before going on.

'Go back. Go back to your camp. Or,' and he paused briefly, for effect, 'or we shall fire the fuses.'

136

For a moment there was chaos around the bridge as the navvies tried to decide whether they had time to rush the tunnel, but Joe stood firm, knowing the strength of his argument. Conor leaned over and put his mouth to Jem's ear.

'I should have guessed. That one would never turn tail. But nor will our men now.' Aloud, he shouted, 'Wait! Let me talk.'

Vaulting off the road on to the earthy slope, he staggered at a run down to the floor of the cutting, with his arms held high and wide to show that he meant no attack. After a brief hesitation, Joe moved forward to speak to him and the two of them began to walk back and forth talking, under the eyes of all the men. Watching tensely, his finger-nails digging into the palms of his hands, Jem could hear the perplexed mutters of the navvies behind him.

Suddenly a convulsive scrabbling broke the anxious quietness. Conor had jumped on Joe. Now the two of them were fighting a desperate battle, half-way between the bridge and the tunnel. No one else moved. For a moment Jem wondered why, and then he realized that the villagers could not leave their guard on the charges and the navvies could not risk the explosion of those charges. So all of them stood and watched. It was an uncanny echo of the fight up at the Copse, but that fight had been almost a game in comparison, with the spectators cheering themselves to hoarseness. Now the fighting was grim and earnest and the watchers kept an eerie silence, so that the only sounds to be heard were the scrape and rattle of stones in the cutting and the call of an owl passing overhead. There were no breaks in this fight, no rounds and no rules.

Conor was a smaller man, and he was sore-headed and weary. From the start he seemed at a disadvantage and even Jem could not believe that he would be able to repeat his victory. But when he saw Joe pin the Irishman to the ground, he knew that Conor *had* to win, that if Conor did not win disaster would come to both the village and the railway. While the smith picked up a stone and grinned round triumphantly, the boy ransacked his head for something to force Conor on, to put him back on his feet.

And the words came. Leaning over the parapet, he screamed as loudly as he could—his voice thin in the stillness—'*He* did it! He wrecked our cottage!'

It was like a match to gunpowder. Conor thrust upwards, taking the smith completely by surprise, and was on his feet and fighting. Both men had been tired, moving slowly, but now the Irishman was fast and fierce. Three times he put Joe on the ground, and the third time the smith groaned and lay still.

The villagers in front of the tunnel began to scutter about agitatedly, consulting together, but none of them made a move and Jem saw suddenly that it was calm calculation and not sheer rage that had made Conor attack Joe. Now, the villagers were leaderless. But was Conor too exhausted and out of breath to take advantage of it? Jem thrust his knuckles hard down on to the rough bricks of the parapet and wished wordlessly.

When Conor did speak, he said the one thing that most of them had forgotten.

'There's men coming up the tunnel,' he shouted. 'Do you want to kill them?'

Jem felt that Joe would have said 'Yes', but without his authority the villagers moved uncertainly. Then, one by one, they started to drift away up the sides of the cutting. Two of them, braver than the rest, came to drag Joe with them and a few of the navvies would have stopped them, but Conor said curtly, without looking backwards, 'Let them be,' and they pulled the heavy body off unmolested. The Irishman ignored everyone except for one man. Walt, the quarryman. He stared steadily at him and, when the pale man tried to follow the villagers, he gestured threateningly to warn him to be still, so that at last he stood alone in front of the mouth of the tunnel, glancing fearfully from side to side.

Feeling that there was nothing now to keep them back, the navvies began to slither down the sides of the cutting, moving nearer to the tunnel. Jem followed them and, by dint of elbowing, found himself close beside Conor. The pale man watched the navvies, his eyes nervously tracing out the half-circle which confronted him. When Conor began to speak again, he started at the noise. Yet the Irishman's voice was soft.

'I've not seen you hereabouts before.'

There was no reply. Only, a wet tongue flicked over the thin lips.

'Are you the quarryman?' Conor snapped out suddenly. The pale man let his head fall forward in a nod.

'Well, now, what are we to do about these charges you've laid? I'm thinking you should be taking them away again. Before the other men come up the tunnel.'

Jem was so close that he could see the sweat gleam on Walt's white-skinned forehead and the fascinated eyes stare at Conor.

'Away with you, now.' Conor's voice was still soft, but there was no mistaking the threat, nor the tension, which showed plainly that he knew the danger in what he was asking. With a last glance around, the quarryman picked up the box at his feet and backed into the thick darkness. As if by common consent, the navvies edged away slightly, leaving enough room for a blast to escape.

Jem stood waiting with the others, listening to the

scraping and rustling noises coming from inside the tunnel. It was so quiet that he could count the breaths of the man on his left and hear the ticking of a watch somewhere on his right. A glance up at Conor showed him that the Irishman was as anxious as the rest of them.

Then the quarryman reappeared and the men in the cutting relaxed audibly. Conor caught Walt by the shoulder.

'Now,' he said coolly, 'shall we see what kind of a job you've done?'

Taking a torch from someone behind him, he propelled the pale man back into the tunnel beside him. The watchers could see the flames of the torch moving about inside the tunnel, up near the roof, down by the floor, swaying from side to side, searching for any forgotten charges or any booby-traps left on purpose. A man behind Jem gave a low whistle of admiration, but not a word was said until Conor and Walt came out of the tunnel. Then, the darkness was split by cheers and wavings of torches. With a contemptuous gesture, Conor motioned to the pale man to make his escape, which he did without a backward glance.

For a while, the navvies milled about aimlessly, congratulating Conor and laughing, and it began to seem that they might be content to go back to the camp. Jem could feel his breathing loosen and he wiped his sweaty forehead with the sleeve of his smock.

Then, in a sudden black rush, the procession that had gone with Pigtail came bursting out of the tunnel. Fearing an explosion, no doubt, they had abandoned their torches and now they emerged bewildered into the flickering light, standing half-blinded while Pigtail shouted, 'Where are the men? Have we come to a nest of mares?'

'Sure, you've missed it all!'

'Kilkenny played them a grand trick!'

'Kilkenny's the lad!'

A hundred voices jostled each other, to tell of Conor's bravery, Conor's cleverness, Conor's strength, and as they spoke Pigtail's dark face tightened unpleasantly. Jem suddenly felt Con's hand clutch warningly at his shoulder and a moment later he guessed the reason as Pigtail threw back his head and bellowed, 'And has Kilkenny got the milk in his liver? The dirty village has threatened us. Has he let the men go?'

There was half a second's pause and then the control of the crowd was loosened. Half the navvies had stood nearly silent for an hour or more, and the others had walked a mile in pitchy darkness. All of them were ready for something fiercer than a quiet walk back to the camp, and now their restraint exploded in cries for revenge.

'Pigtail's right!'

'We'll learn them to play games with us!'

'To the village!'

Conor bent down to Jem and whispered in his ear, 'Quickly. Be off and warn the village.'

But, dazed by the turnabout in the crowd's mood, Jem hesitated briefly, and in that second Pigtail saw him.

'The boy! The village boy! Hold him!'

A dozen pairs of hands clutched at Jem's body and clothing, until he could not have moved an inch, and he became a helpless observer. It looked as if the crowd might sweep away at once to the village with no check to their enthusiasm, but Conor jumped on to a rock and shouted at them.

'Stop!'

They jeered and grumbled, but the memory of what he had done was strong in at least half of them and they gave him a grudging silence.

'What about the women? The children?' His voice echoed, over their heads, in the bare cutting. 'Have they done you harm, that you'd come on them in their beds in the night, like wild heathen?'

They muttered at him, uncertain of what to say, and he tried to take hold of this mood. 'There's no harm yet. The tunnel's saved. Set guards on it. But don't risk prison or worse. Not for a handful of mud-grubbers.'

The men shuffled and murmured and Jem held his breath. Perhaps Conor had done it. Perhaps their respect for him had saved the village. But he hoped too soon. Pigtail's voice sounded mockingly above the murmurs.

'Poor Kilkenny! Afraid for your woman in the village?'

A shout of laughter broke the tension that Conor had forced on them, sweeping away his reasoning. Pigtail needed no further argument to sway the men to his side. At his 'Come on!' they surged forward. No one held Jem now, but he went with them unavoidably, unable to think of anything but keeping his feet in the torrent of bodies. Away to his left he could see Conor's head in the crowd, but he could not make towards him. And anyway what could the two of them have done? Only, as they ran, Jem said over and over in his head, 'Please, please, please, PLEASE.' Something must happen. Something must save the village.

The navvies raced on in almost total darkness, broken here and there by an occasional remaining torch, and as they ran they sent up a humming like a swarm of bees, made up of each man's abuse of the village. Across the side of the Beacon they swept and down the twisting path towards the village, their feet scrambling and scraping on the chalk.

But, as they came round the last bend, into the open space at the edge of the village, the navvies in front stopped suddenly and those behind them cannoned together. The shock of the sudden halt sent Jem staggering forwards and he used this to push his way to the front of the crowd, anxious to know what was happening. It was a moment before he was steady enough to look about him, but when he did he saw the reason for the halt and he nearly shouted with relief. It was only the forethought of the village men, maybe, but to him at that moment it seemed like the hand of God.

The villagers were strung out in a line across the whole edge of the village, lantern-light flickering on gunbarrels and reaping hooks, and the cold night wind ruffling the shawls of the women who stood behind. No sound came from any of them. Five yards ahead of the line stood a solitary and commanding figure. Dazed as he was, Jem thought at first that it must be Joe, and wondered how the smith could have recovered so quickly. Then he saw who it really was. It was the Rector. He stood in front of his parishioners with a steady stillness Jem had never seen in him before and, when the navvies bumped to a halt twenty yards away, he shouted, 'Now!'

The shots were uneven, but impressive. Taken completely by surprise the crowd of navvies seethed and panted like a huge, unpredictable animal. For the first time that he could remember, Jem felt afraid of them. Across the empty space he could see Kate's shawl flutter as she stood there with Martha in her arms, and he wished that he were beside her.

Mr Neville took a step forward. 'What do you want?'

A confusion of talk rose from the navvies, until Pigtail

was pushed forward to act as spokesman. He addressed himself to Mr Neville, but shouted what he had to say in a loud voice, so that everyone could hear.

'They have tried to explode our tunnel. We have come to fire their village. Is fair.' From behind him came a noise of agreement which went on until Mr Neville held up his hand for silence.

'You did right,' his voice rang through the darkness, 'to guard your work. But you do wrong to attack other men's homes.' A few straggling boos greeted this, but his parson's voice rose effortlessly above them. 'We shot above your heads, but if you attack we shall shoot at your hearts. And we shall kill at least ten of you.'

It was an overestimate. Jem knew that at least half the guns hardly worked at all. But the navvies were impressed. They hung back, not daring to risk the shots, but unable to go. It was as if they needed something to save their embarrassment, so that they should not simply slink home like frightened children. It was Pigtail who found it for them.

'We have come too late!' he shouted suddenly. 'We have talked too long at the tunnel!'

The men caught his meaning at once, eager for someone to blame, but he went on shouting to make sure that everyone understood. 'Kilkenny! He has kept us talking!'

It was what they had been waiting for. Suddenly, the anger of the huge crowd turned away from the village and the navvies caught hold of Conor and began to drag him away up the Beacon, shouting their fury at him.

At that moment, all Jem could feel was relief that the village was saved. He sank to his knees and buried his face in his hands, exhausted. But sharp fingers dug suddenly into his arm.

'Jem! Jem!'

144

It was Kate, distraught and wild-haired, with the baby on her hip.

'Jem, where are they going?'

His head was muzzy. 'Don't know. Don't care.'

'You fool!' Her face was dark, and she was shouting at him. 'Conor! They've taken Conor!'

Then, at last, he realized what he had just seen—Conor, dragged off by a mob of enemies. He got slowly to his feet, but Kate had already run past him, after the navvies who were still streaming up the Beacon. He saw her catch a straggler by the sleeve, talking earnestly. The man shrugged, pointed and turned away. Running back down the hill, Kate shouted without ceremony at the backs of the departing villagers, 'Don't go! Come on! They're going to kill Mr O'Flynn!'

But the only answer was shrugs and head-shakings as the men picked up their weapons and started home. Kate caught at one of them.

'Mr Funnell. You must help. They'll kill him.'

'Now, my dear,'—Ted Funnell had known her since she was a child—'let them be. They've seen enough of us tonight. The man will come to no harm.'

'But—' she began to protest, but the men took no notice of her. For them it was all over.

Kate thrust the baby into Jem's arms. 'Here. I must tell Mr Neville. *He'll* make them come.'

Her face was desperate, her hair falling in long strands over her shoulders, and she spoke to Jem almost as though she could not see him. He followed her dumbly to where Mr Neville stood stooped, with his back to them.

'Oh, sir, *please!*' She bobbed a perfunctory curtsy. 'You must get the men to come. They'll kill Mr O'Flynn.'

Mr Neville made a muffled, indistinct noise, without turning, and Kate took it for a question.

'If you please, sir, he's the navigator used to lodge with me, and—' but at that moment the Rector turned and she stopped, seeing his face. He did not look in the least like a man who had just outfaced an army of navvies. He was white and shaking, almost as though he were about to be sick. Jem remembered, remorsefully, all the jokes about his nervous stomach.

But Kate was merciless in her desperation. 'Mr Neville. Mr *Neville*. You'll help me, won't you? There's a man like to be killed.'

With an effort, he raised his face to look at her and spoke, weakly but kindly. 'Catherine, if we chase after them it will never end. And what could we do? Let them settle their quarrels themselves, my dear. The man will come to no harm.'

Kate snorted. 'You're afraid. Like all of them.'

'That's enough.' Hoppy Noyce had hobbled up unnoticed, and now he ranged himself beside the Rector. 'Rector got out of his bed to save us all from Joe Hamage's foolishness. And from our own. He's done enough for one night.'

He ushered Mr Neville away almost protectively. As they went, Kate screamed after them, 'It was Conor saved the village!' but they did not listen. Sinking to her knees in the damp grass, she buried her face and began to cry, with sobs that shook her whole body. Jem squatted awkwardly beside her, balancing the baby precariously.

'Aw, Kate, don't take on. It will be fine, you'll see. Conor can take care of himself.'

His voice roused her and she looked up bitterly. 'Against all them?'

'He'll be all right.' He hoped it was true. In any case, he did not see what else they could do and his whole body ached, selfishly, for sleep.

But Kate shook herself and got to her feet. 'Give me the child. You take the lantern.'

He went back to pick it up and then suddenly saw which way she was heading.

'Kate!'

'Come on,' she said fiercely. 'The tunnel's where they've gone. Where they can hold off an army till they've done with him.'

'But we can't—'

She rounded on him. 'Are you telling me he's none of ours? You too?'

'But what can we do?'

'We can *find* him!' She stumped away up the hill, leaving him to follow or not, as he chose. For a moment he stared after her, his mouth dry with fear and then, slowly, he began to climb.

CHAPTER THIRTEEN

By the time they reached the bridge over the line, it was coming on to dawn and, looking up the cutting in the first light, they could see the dark shape of the windmill on the hill above the tunnel entrance. The mouth of the tunnel showed as a darker shape in the darkness of the side of the hill.

The cutting was utterly deserted and, looking down at it from the bridge, Jem could hardly believe that it was such a short time since he had seen it ringed with lights while two men struggled there.

Kate left him no time to think of that. Clutching the baby with one hand and her skirts with the other, she scrambled and slithered down the slope, calling to him to follow with the lantern. Her boots crunched on the floor of the cutting and her hair, escaped completely from its pins, hung down her back in a tangled mass. She looked like one of the tally-women. As he came up with her at the mouth of the tunnel, Jem could only admire her relentlessness. The thought of what might be in the tunnel hung like a dark shadow in his mind.

'Do you think . . . they're still there?'

She shrugged. 'Maybe. It's Conor I've come for.'

Her bony back was stiff and straight and her jaw set firm, and Jem gained a smattering of courage from the sight of her as they walked into the tunnel. Inside, the darkness was total and, but for the lantern, they would not have been able to see even their feet in front of them. Jem lifted it high and the light struck on the walls and roof but showed only a little of the way ahead, so that they moved on cautiously, hearing nothing but the scrunching of their own boots. Kate began to call out, softly at first and then louder.

'Mr O'Flynn! Conor!'

Her voice echoed eerily in the empty tunnel, but no other sound came in answer.

'Conor!'

Jem shivered in the coldness. He could not believe that they would really find Conor, but he added his voice to hers, for company as much as anything.

'Kilkenny, are you there?'

'Conor!'

'Kilkenny! Con!'

Searching and calling, they moved a hundred yards or so up the tunnel.

'Conor!'

Suddenly they heard a faint noise, and Kate gripped Jem's arm fiercely. Someone had answered their calling. They hurried on and found, not Conor, but Ginger, slumped on the floor, with a dark trickle of blood running into his eyes. He raised his head with an attempt at a smile.

'Might have known it would be you, Miss Penfold.'

'Conor?' Kate bent over him urgently.

'Did what I could,' he wheezed, 'but they knocked me cold.'

'Where's Conor?'

'Give us an arm.'

Leaning on Jem, Ginger staggered to his feet and stumbled with them up the tunnel. A hundred yards further on he stopped and pointed.

'Must be there. Poor devil.'

Just ahead a black heap lay to one side of the tunnel, huddled up against the wall. Jem could hardly bear to go on, fearful of what he might find, but Ginger's fingers on his arm pressed him painfully forward and they came up to the heap.

He lay with his eyes closed, his hair matted with blood which streaked his forehead and ran down one side of his face. The awkward twist of his legs showed at a glance that they were both broken.

'God help us all,' muttered Ginger, 'he's dead.'

But Kate, impatiently thrusting the baby at Jem, knelt down and put her hand on his face.

'Conor? It's Kate.'

The heavy eyelids flickered open, closed again and then slowly raised until Conor was looking up at them from dulled eyes. Incredibly, a ghost of his old, teasing smile came over his face and he said, his voice cracked and almost inaudible, 'You're a lovely girl, Kate Penfold.'

When she spoke again, there was a catch in her voice. 'What have they done to you? Who was it?'

They all leaned closer to distinguish his reply. What he said was, 'Let it be. Let it be, my dear.'

'But we can't—' Kate was almost crying.

Conor forced himself to go on speaking. 'This . . . could be an end . . . if you only . . . let it be.'

Exhausted, he closed his eyes and allowed his head to fall back. Kate took hold of his hand and said urgently, 'Jem, get up to the village and find someone to come with a hurdle.'

'Who?' He sounded foolish, but he could not think of anyone. The villagers had refused already, and the navvies would surely never come. Who was left?

Kate considered for a moment and then—'Miss Ellen. Go to her. She'll help us.'

Lantern, baby and all, Jem stumbled back up the tunnel, leaving Kate, Conor and Ginger in the darkness. He was so tired that everything had taken on the substance of a dream and his legs moved mechanically on their errand. When Martha woke and began to cry he rocked her unthinkingly in his arm. She was a heavy weight to carry now and too late he thought that he should have left her with Kate. But it made no difference. Plodding and jogging alternately, he made his way as quickly as he could over the mile to the village. The morning was cold and bleak and the birds were twittering fretfully, as though eager for the sunrise. As he went, he tried to plan what he would say, but the only words that came into his head were 'Conor. In the tunnel.' Con is in the tun-nel. Con is in the tun-nel. His feet heaved themselves along to the rhythm as if it meant nothing, his mind shying away from the reality as the horse had swerved away at the raw end of the cutting. Time enough to think later.

The village lane was empty and he was grateful for it, not wanting to meet anyone who might ask him questions. Con is in the tun-nel. Past the bakehouse. Past the forge. Con is in the tun-nel. The Rectory was at the far end, past the church, and by the time he reached it he was staggering. The baby wailed in the cold air, but he was too tired to rock her any more.

He lurched round to the back door and heaved on the bellrope, setting the heavy iron bell swinging. Then, exhausted, he leaned on the door and must have dozed for a second, for when it finally opened he fell straight into the arms of Mary Ann.

'Lord save us!' She sounded amazed and, sleepily, he thought how strange it was to see her in her white nightgown, a long grey plait over one shoulder. She propelled him to a chair by the cold fireplace and stood back to look at him.

'Jem Penfold! What are you doing getting decent folks out of their beds?'

'Con is in the tunnel.' But it meant nothing to her.
'What are you saying?'

Jem tried to drag his mind awake. 'Miss Ellen. I must see Miss Ellen.'

'At this time in the morning? Are you out of your mind? I'm sure I can't—'

'Miss Ellen.'

Mary Ann looked at him sharply. 'All right. I'll see. Give me the baby.'

She took Martha and the lantern and Jem fell asleep instantly, where he sat.

'Good morning, Jem.'

He had slept for perhaps ten minutes and now he dragged himself awake desperately. Miss Ellen was standing in front of him, calm and dressed, her face full of concern. He opened his mouth and the words came out of their own accord.

'Con is in the tunnel.'

'Con? Who is Con?'

'That lodged with us.'

'The navvy?'

He nodded heavily and she sat down on a chair beside him and took his hand.

'What do you want from me? I can't help unless you tell me. Try now.'

His tongue thick and stumbling, he told her as best he could and she nodded quickly, picking up the story with wonderful quickness. Obviously she knew something of the night's events.

'All right, Jem, I'll see what I can do. Mary Ann!'

'Yes, Miss Ellen?' Mary Ann was disapproving but obedient.

'Would you be so good as to give the boy some bread and a drink? I'll be back in ten minutes.'

When she had rustled away, Mary Ann, rumbling and

muttering about 'midnight goings-on', gave Jem some bread and a cup of milk and set the baby in a chair with a crust to gnaw.

It was wheaten bread, spread with Mary Ann's famous butter, and at any other time it would have been a treat. But now Jem ate it as if it were chaff. Nevertheless, it made him feel stronger and he was just beginning to lift his head and look around when a voice broke in on him.

'And *what* is going on?'

Mrs Neville was standing, majestic and threatening, in the kitchen doorway. 'Why are you feeding village boys in the middle of the night, Mary Ann?'

'Please 'm,' said Mary Ann, only too anxious to dissociate herself from the whole affair, 'Miss Ellen's orders.'

'Miss *Ellen*?' Mrs Neville turned to Jem. 'You, boy, what is all this about?'

Jem's mouth opened, but no sound came. Instead, from behind Mrs Neville, a voice said firmly, 'He came to ask my help, Mamma, and I am going to give it.'

'This is most improper, Ellen. Kindly send him about his business.' Mrs Neville turned to leave, as though it did not occur to her that she would not be obeyed.

'No, Mamma. I am going to rescue an injured man from the tunnel.' Miss Ellen's face was calm and her voice as cool and controlled as her father's when he faced the navvies. 'Are you ready, Jem? The men are waiting with the hurdle.'

'Ellen, I absolutely *forbid* you to go!'

Miss Ellen motioned Jem towards the door, taking no notice of her mother until they had nearly gone. Then, turning back to the kitchen, she said quietly, 'I think you will find that father agrees with me.'

And they were gone, incredibly.

The two men who held the hurdle were the Benson brothers from down the lane. They smiled rather sheepishly at Jem, obviously embarrassed by their errand, and he gave them as friendly a nod as he could manage. But it was not a journey for conversation. He led the way in silence.

As soon as they saw Kate, they knew that he was dead. She stood in the tunnel-opening, dwarfed by the arch over her head, with her loose hair falling on her shoulders and her shawl wrapped tightly round her. She did not move as they slid down into the cutting and walked along towards her and they stopped a few feet away, awed by her stillness. She stared not at them, but at the hurdle.

Miss Ellen stepped forward and touched her on the arm. 'Catherine?'

'He's dead,' Kate said dully. 'In the tunnel.'

Miss Ellen made a move, as if she would have caught the other girl in her arms, but Kate turned away and lifted a hand to call the men after her into the tunnel.

Jem watched them go. He did not want to see the inside of the tunnel again, nor the crumpled body huddled against the wall. Con could not be dead. Last night he had been alive and shouting. The night before, he and Jem had shared the same bed and planned a new life for them all. Pictures whirled through Jem's mind and abruptly he turned his back on the tunnel.

Miss Ellen gave his arm a sympathetic touch, but she did not speak, did not offer the false condolences and moralizing that her mother would have thought necessary. Glancing up, Jem saw that her face was tense and miserable.

When they brought the hurdle out of the tunnel, there was nothing terrible to see after all. Only an anonymous body. Kate had spread her shawl over Conor's head and shoulders so that no one could see his dead face and she followed the hurdle, supporting the limping Ginger. When they came up to the others, Jem lent his shoulder to Ginger and Miss Ellen put her arm round Kate and led her after the hurdle, towards the village.

Until they were almost there Kate allowed them to lead her, but, as they approached the last bend, she suddenly stepped away and walked on her own beside the hurdle, her head held proudly high.

Rounding the corner, Jem suddenly saw that her instinct for ceremony had been right. The villagers stood along both sides of the lane, the children quiet and the men bare-headed in respect, to watch Kate Penfold bring home the body of Conor O'Flynn. Mr Neville stood nearest them and, as the hurdle passed, he fell into step beside Kate. Behind the hurdle Jem walked with Ginger and Miss Ellen and after them the village began to follow, two by two, until they formed a long procession. So, solemnly and silently, the men and women of the village followed the body of a navvy.

And when they reached the lych-gate of the church, the first rays of the rising sun struck golden over the Beacon.

CHAPTER FOURTEEN

Kate did not speak for three days. Not to Jem, not to Ginger before he went back up to the camp, not even to Mr Neville and Miss Ellen, who wanted to look after her. She scrubbed the cottage, washed and fed the baby, and did her sewing as usual, but the only sound that broke the quiet was the baby's crying and the clatter of pans. At first Jem tried to persuade her to talk about what had happened, but her eyes roamed vaguely over his head and, in the end, he left her alone.

The villagers did the same to both of them. There were sympathetic glances in plenty, but everyone seemed to feel a shyness about speaking, and Jem did not like to begin it himself. He felt almost as if it were indecent to speak to outsiders of what had happened. Only to Ginger could he have spoken, and Ginger was up at the camp again. Jem felt that nothing could ever drag him back to the camp.

But on the third day he could stand the silence no longer. As he walked home from work he decided that he must talk to someone. But whom? Miss Ellen, Mr Neville, even Mary Ann probably, would make him welcome, give him a drink of tea and talk politely, but politeness was not what he needed. He needed the company of someone of his own kind, who would understand what he had been feeling. Almost before he had thought it all out he found his footsteps taking him towards the forge and, although he could feel his old fear of the smith creeping over him as he went up the path, his fear of never breaking the silence was stronger. He lifted his hand and knocked at the half-open door.

When the smith put his head round he looked smaller, older. Jem found that he could look him in the eye and that Joe's eyes fell away first.

'I want Ben,' he said boldly, and waited to be sent about his business with a roar. But the roar did not come. Joe jerked his head towards the cottage and disappeared back to his work. Jem went on and knocked at the kitchen door.

Ben opened the door and at once went rigid, his eyes wary.

'Your dad said you were here,' said Jem quickly.

'Oh?'

Jem dug his boot-tip into the earth of the path. 'Fancy a walk up the bridge?'

'Could do.'

The two boys paced side by side, silently, with their hands deep in their trouser pockets, until they stood in the middle of the little stone bridge. For a moment they leaned on the stonework, gazing down at the little stream which idled over the pebbles. Then Ben gulped.

'A bad business that. The other night.'

'Yes.' Jem bent down and picked up a handful of little stones. He began to toss them one by one into the water. At last he went on. 'The crowner's court sits tomorrow.'

'To find who did it?'

Jem shrugged. 'Does it matter?' Then he looked sideways and saw the apprehension on Ben's face. 'Not your dad,' he said quickly, generously. 'They'll only care for them that struck the blows.' He tossed another stone. 'And what does it matter? It wasn't them. It was everyone killed him really.' He felt as he had when he had fought and beaten Ben in the darkness. Not all the revenge in the world would heal what had happened.

'My dad said—' Ben stopped timidly, but went on when he saw Jem's questioning glance. 'My dad said last night that he was a brave man. That he wished it hadn't happened.'

It was in the nature of a peace offering and Jem accepted it with a nod. Then, suddenly, he tossed the rest of his stones into the water and shouted aloud, 'Oh, why did they ever come?'

The next day he and Kate went to the Coroner's Court. It did not seem to have very much to do with what had happened. They both answered questions and told all that they knew, Kate's voice sounding hoarse and rusty from her long silence, but no one came forward to tell any more and the jury found that Conor had been murdered by unknown persons. Then they went home.

That made a kind of end to it all. Kate and Jem took up more or less the life they had led before Conor came, working hard and scraping for halfpennies. Jem took his turn in the fields every day, glad that there was work to do, and in the evening he went down to the forge to see Ben. But he never went to watch the work on the line any more and, although he felt ungrateful, he never ventured up to the camp to ask after Ginger. As far as he could, he tried to pretend that the navvies had never come and that he had never heard of the railway. Only sometimes, when he heard the villagers talking in the forge and saying that the line was nearly finished, his heart ached for the foolishness of it all and the waste of Conor's death. But he tried not to think of the railway.

He had almost grown accustomed once more to the bleak life he and Kate led alone together when he came home from work one day to find Miss Ellen in the cottage. Until then, she had respected Kate's need for silence, merely smiling at her in church and indicating that help was there if Kate should need it. Now she stood beside the fire, with a touch of her old diffidence, and as Jem came in she said, 'You're sure you won't change your mind, Kate?'

'No thank you, Miss Ellen. You mean kindly, I'm sure, but I'd not feel easy with all the grand folks.'

Jem looked up questioningly and Miss Ellen said, 'It's the official opening of the railway tomorrow. I came to ask Kate if you would both like to go to Helmston and see it.' But he shook his head silently. Miss Ellen lowered her eyes for a moment and then went on, 'The other thing is—I went up to the navvies' camp. To see how Ginger was.'

'Up at Fat Maggie's?' Jem could hardly believe it, and she laughed at his gaping face.

'Yes, I went to Fat Maggie's.' Then she turned to Kate. 'He gave me these things. He said that Conor said you were to have them.'

'Yes,' said Kate slowly, reaching out her hand. 'Yes. In the tunnel.'

'Well, Ginger sent them. With his good wishes.'

The sight of the battered bundle, wrapped in a blue handkerchief, seemed to have paralysed Kate. She stood staring at it as Miss Ellen tipped it into her outstretched hands, and did not even seem to hear her visitor gently saying goodbye and leaving. Her eyes were locked to what she held.

'Aren't you going to look at it?' asked Jem at last, less out of curiosity than because her silence frightened him. Still without a word, she sat down at the table and opened the bundle. Inside, there were two things: a lumpy stocking and something long and thin, wrapped in a piece of rag. Picking up the stocking, she turned it upside-down and tipped the money on to the table. The heap of golden sovereigns lay strangely on the bare wood of the table. More than Jem had ever seen. More than he had ever thought of. He and Kate looked at them for a long time, well aware of what they meant. Food. Freedom. Warmth. There was enough to keep the three of them out of the shadow of the workhouse for ever. But all that Jem could think was that it was a poor exchange for Conor. Glancing sideways at Kate, he could see that she was thinking the same and he watched her fingers as they picked up each coin separately and slid it back into the stocking. When the top of the stocking was twisted into a knot, the fingers reached out for the other thing from the bundle and began to unwrap the rag. There, in Kate's hands, lay Conor's silver whistle and, at the sight of it, she bent down her head and, at last, started to cry.

She said nothing, that night, about Conor, but the next morning she tied on her green and purple bonnet that he had given her and held out to Jem his best smock.

'Get this on you.'

'But where are we—'

'To watch the first train on the line.'

'But you told Miss Ellen—'

Kate shrugged. 'Could be I've changed my mind. Anyway, we'll be best off in our own place, with no grand folks to worry about.'

Jem pulled the smock over his head. 'Where'll we go, then?' For a moment Kate hesitated and then she lowered her eyelids before replying.

'We'll go up to the bridge. By the tunnel.'

It was a hot day. The white dust from the road covered their good boots with a misty bloom and the green blades of the barley showed on the other side of the hedge. Kate set Martha down to crawl for a while and she and Jem ambled along the road, between hedgerows sprinkled with clumps of yellow primroses. Almost absentmindedly, Kate began to pick the primroses, until her hands were full. Then, all at once, she seemed to panic about being late.

'Carry the baby a step, Jem.'

'Aw, Kate, she's like a load of turnip.'

'Come on. Or we'll miss seeing the train.'

Grumbling, Jem heaved Martha up on to his hip and they went on at a faster pace until they got to the cutting. The bridge was already well-sprinkled with people, most of them strangers, crowding the parapet and looking towards the tunnel. A few of them must have recognized Kate, for they cleared a way for the three Penfolds.

Kate and Jem leaned on the stonework of the bridge and looked up the cutting. It had changed since they saw it last. Now, the new rails flung the sun back into their eyes and the threatening black hole of the tunnel-mouth was dwarfed by the turrets and crenellations built round it. Jem felt a sick sense of loss. A year ago he would have been gripping the bridge with excitement at the thought of seeing a train come along those rails on its way to London. But his excitement had been betrayed. He turned his head away and, suddenly angry with Kate, muttered fiercely under his breath, 'What did we come here for? How could you come?'

She gazed down the line, a crinkle between her eyes, and said softly at last, 'He loved the railway.'

'I loved it too!' Jem's voice was bitter. 'But it killed him.'

'No.' She was running her finger thoughtfully along the stone parapet. 'I thought that. But it wasn't the railway. It was the strangeness of the navvies. Them being incomers.' She paused for a moment and then went on, with a diffidence Jem had never seen before in her. 'Perhaps . . . perhaps the railway will help to do away with that. Perhaps it will take away the strangeness.'

She looked towards him for agreement, but he lowered his eyes, uncertain, and she suddenly cried out, 'He can't have died for *nothing*!'

'Maybe not,' muttered Jem. It was all he could bring himself to say, but as he looked along the line again he felt a quick stirring of excitement.

The other spectators were beginning to move restlessly, pulling out their watches and comparing the times.

'Won't be long now.'

'Five minutes. No more.'

Craning forward, they peered into the blackness of the tunnel as if they were awaiting a miracle, and Jem suddenly caught their sense of its being a great occasion.

'I wish we *had* gone with Miss Ellen,' he burst out.

'Listen.' Kate gripped his arm painfully. 'Do you know what all those grand folks are saying? They're making fine speeches to thank the engineer and the men that put in the money. As if it was them made the railway.'

'Didn't they?' Jem rubbed his arm sulkily.

'It wasn't them that sweated. It wasn't them that died. It was men like Ginger and . . . and Kilkenny Con built it, with picks and shovels and hard work. But who's to remember? Only us.'

They could hear the noise in the tunnel now, and they strained forwards with all the others to catch the first sight of the train. A shout went up from the watchers on the cutting slopes and a cloud of steam billowed out of the blackness. Then a roar, and the train poured out, on and on and on, as if it would never stop, rattling up the cutting towards the bridge, while the passengers waved flags, handkerchiefs, bonnets, and the watchers waved back, cheering and hurrahing.

As the train began to run under the bridge Kate, standing like an island of quiet in the general roar, leant deliberately out over the parapet and began to scatter the primroses from her hand in a shower upon the roofs of the carriages. Some blew off straight away, but others travelled on with the train. Picking up the baby who crawled at her feet, Kate crossed the bridge with the other watchers and they stood looking at the train as it swayed and clattered along the line, away to London. Most of the spectators were cheering still, but Kate and Jem stood silently, watching the noisy train, with its load of bright, springtime yellow, and then the rails, left suddenly clear, pointing brightly into the distance.

OTHER BOOKS BY GILLIAN CROSS

Calling a Dead Man

ISBN 0 19 271827 4

How did John Cox die? His sister Hayley thinks she knows, but she wants to see the place where it happened. With John's friend Annie she travels to Russia to visit the site of the explosion that killed him. But they soon realize that there is more to John's death that meets the eye. And certain people are desperate to keep them from finding out the truth.

Meanwhile, deep in the wastes of Siberia, a man with no memory and a high fever stumbles out of the forest . . .

Tightrope

ISBN 0 19 271750 2

Eddie Beale looks after his friends, people say, as long as they entertain him. When he takes notice of Ashley, she is happy to put on a show and be part of the excitement that surrounds him and his gang—it is a relief from the unrelenting drudgery of her life. Then she realizes that someone is watching her. Someone is stalking her and leaving messages that get uglier and uglier. Can Eddie help her? And if he does, what price will she have to pay?

The Great Elephant Chase

ISBN 0 19 271786 3

Winner of the Smarties Prize and the
Whitbread Children's Novel Award

The elephant changed their lives for ever. Because of the elephant,
Tad and Cissie become entangled in a chase across America, by
train, by flatboat and steam boat. Close behind is Hannibal Jackson,
who is determined to have the elephant for himself. And how do you
hide an enormous Indian elephant?

'An undoubted classic.'
The Sunday Times

Wolf

ISBN 0 19 271784 7
Winner of the Carnegie Medal

Cassy hears sinister footsteps in the middle of the night. Suddenly
she is packed off to stay with her beautiful feckless mother. There is
no explanation. Something has gone frighteningly wrong.

Danger is coming after Cassy. And behind it lurks the dark
wolf-shape that seems to slink into everything.

Even her dreams.

'An outstanding achievement.'
The Times Educational Supplement

New World

ISBN 0 19 271852 5

Miriam is delighted when she is asked to test a new virtual reality game. She's not so thrilled with Stuart, her partner in the test, but once they're inside the game she forgets their differences and the outside world completely.

Then things start to go wrong. Something—or someone—is playing on the deepest fears of Miriam and Stuart. Could this be a part of the test? Or is there someone else in the game?

'A new Gillian Cross novel is always a treat, and *New World* is no exception.'
Sunday Telegraph

'a tour-de-force'
The Financial Times

On the Edge

ISBN 0 19 271863 0

It hit him out of the blue. He was exhausted and unprepared. An arm around his neck, a hand over his mouth. His brain was telling him to fight—but he had nothing left.

Tug wakes up in a strange house with strange people—but why have they chosen him? And why are they trying to mess with his head? He's not even sure who he is any more . . .

His only hope is that someone will save him in time—before it comes to the crunch and he is forced to decide his own destiny.

The Dark Behind the Curtain

ISBN 0 19 275149 2

Jackus hates being in the school play. But once the rehearsals begin, he starts feeling frightened, too. Inexplicable things are happening and it's hard to tell when people are acting and when they're not.

A disaster threatens. Can nobody else see it but Jackus? Has he got the courage to stop it—or will he have to watch the others play out the tragedy to the end?

A Map of Nowhere

ISBN 0 19 275154 9

Nick is intrigued by the mysterious note he finds in his bag. It looks like strange instructions for some kind of adventure game. He is determined to find out more and join in the game.

But soon his loyalties are put to the test. When he's really up against it, he has to decide whether to carry on playing games, or to stand up for what he knows is right.

Chartbreak

ISBN 0 19 275153 0

Finch is alone in a motorway café. She's left home. A scruffy bunch of lads are on the next table. They say they're a rock band. Finch can sing. And she does. Then and there, in the café.

Next thing, she's in the band.
Discovered!

But even as fame arrives, there's still the brooding menace of Christie, the lead singer.

Is it hate—or something else . . .

Born of the Sun

ISBN 0 19 275151 4

It's a dream come true! After years of planning, Paula and her father are off to South America—to find a lost Inca city.

The dream turns into a nightmare. As they descend into the jungle, Paula begins to suspect that something is terribly wrong. Why is her father so impatient? Why is he acting so strange? Are they really being followed? What begins as an exciting expedition suddenly begins to look very dangerous indeed . . .

Roscoe's Leap

ISBN 0 19 275150 6

Roscoe's Leap—for Hannah it's just the huge, decaying house where she lives with her brother Stephen. But for Stephen himself, it's a place of secrets. A place where something happened to him long ago—something dark and terrifying which lies just outside of his memory.

Then a history student arrives at the house and starts to uncover its mysteries. And the terror that has slept so long in Stephen's mind begins to stir again . . .

Pictures in the Dark

ISBN 0 19 271741 3

When Charlie takes the photograph of the unknown animal swimming in the river that night, he has no idea of the effect it will have on his life.

Why is Peter, the boy with the strange, staring eyes, so obsessed by the picture? And what is it about Peter that upsets everybody so much—even his own father? When Charlie tries to help Peter and protect him from the bullying, he is led deeper into the secret, mysterious life of the river bank, and the creatures that inhabit it.